SHOW TIME!

Not For Blondes Only:

Five's a Crowd

Show Time!

NOT FOR BLONDES ONLY

SHOW TIME!

Betsy Lifton and Karen Lifton

AN
APPLE
PAPERBACK

SCHOLASTIC INC.
New York Toronto London Auckland Sydney

ISBN 0-590-45683-0

12 11 10 9 8 7 6 5 4 3 2 1   2 3 4 5 6 7/9

Printed in the U.S.A.   28

First Scholastic printing, August 1992

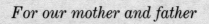

For our mother and father

SHOW TIME!

1

"Pam! Ouch! That hurts!"

Abby Wagner was sitting on a stool with her head in the bathroom sink while Pamela Baldwin massaged mayonnaise into Abby's strawberry-blonde hair. It was a Sunday afternoon, and the Not For Blondes Only club was hanging around Pamela's enormous bathroom. We'd tried lemon juice a couple of times to lighten our hair, but this was the first time we'd let Pam experiment on us with different beauty treatments. And probably the last time.

"If you'd stop wriggling around so much, I wouldn't have to pull," said Pam.

"Yeah, well, if you'd stop pulling, I wouldn't have to wriggle," Abby muttered.

"Whose idea was this, anyway?" I asked. I'm Beth Hanson. I was sitting on the edge of the toilet with my hands soaking in a disgusting mishmash of grape jelly and lemon juice.

"Not mine," said Kate Tucker, who lay on the

floor, covered from head to toe in Pam's home-made honey-and-granola mask.

"Stop complaining, you guys," Pam said. "We have to sit here until the phone rings, *anyway*, so we may as well do something constructive."

I wasn't completely convinced that smearing the entire contents of the Baldwins' refrigerator all over ourselves could really be considered constructive, but I didn't want to hurt Pam's feelings by saying so. Besides, it was probably better than *eating* the entire contents of the Baldwins' refrigerator.

"What is it o'clock?" asked Sarah Stern, the newest member, and the only brunette, in the club. She was lying squished up in Pam's empty bathtub with slices of cucumber on her face, and strawberry yogurt slathered all over her long, skinny legs.

"Only twelve-thirty," I said.

I love the way Sarah says stuff like, "What is it o'clock?" She has such an odd and interesting way of putting things. I think she gets a lot of it from the old-fashioned romance novels she's always reading. When Abby first became friends with her, Pam and Kate thought she was a dorfball because of the way she speaks. I have to admit, I kind of felt that way, too. But, now, sometimes when I'm by myself at home, I actually try to say things the way I think she would. I always sound pretty stupid. She doesn't, though. She just sounds absolutely original.

"Five more hours," moaned Kate.

"You guys, it's nuts to sit here for five more hours," Abby said from the sink. "Let's go to the mall. Ready Freddy is not going to call."

Ready Freddy is the D.J. on WROK, our favorite radio station here in South Meadow, Connecticut. That day, the station was having a contest. A few weeks before, you had to mail in a postcard with your phone number on it. Then, that Sunday, Ready Freddy was going to pick a card at random and call the person who'd sent it. If that person answered the phone "WROK — where you pick the hits," he'd win a WROK T-shirt, a fifty-dollar gift certificate to Music Plus, and the chance to be a D.J. for a day. The only problem was that Ready Freddy could call anytime before five o'clock, so you had to sit at home all day long, waiting for the phone to ring. And, so far, it hadn't even rung once.

"You never know, Abby," I said. "Anything can happen." Even though we'd sent in about a million postcards with Pam's number, I didn't really believe that, and, truthfully, I had other stuff to be doing myself. Mr. MacFadden, the absolutely coolest and handsomest teacher in all of South Meadow Middle School, was holding auditions for *Alice in Wonderland* on Monday, and since I was trying out for the part of Alice, I should have been home, reading the script and thinking about the character. But Pam and Kate wanted to win this contest more than anything. Pam had even decided to stay at home instead of going with her parents to a fancy restaurant in the city. So, since we'd all agreed to do it, I felt that I should keep my word.

I was also afraid that if I tried to leave early, Pam would get upset, and I didn't want that. I absolutely hate to start a fight. Even the smallest argument makes me queasy, and I always feel as if it's my job to make everything okay again.

Take the big blowup that the club had when Abby got to be friends with Sarah. It all seems really stupid now, but for a while there, things were pretty awful. You see, back then we called our club For Blondes Only, and it was just Pamela, Abby, Kate, and me. Pam had made up the name when we were about eight, because we were best friends and we all happened to have blonde hair.

Then Abby became friends with Sarah, but Pam and Kate thought she was too dorfy to be in the club. I have to admit, I kind of agreed. We thought she was really odd, and didn't understand that that's what makes her so special. We had a big fight, and I was worried we were going to wind up enemies for life. But at last we all realized we were being jerks. So Pam renamed the club *Not* For Blondes Only, and now Sarah's a member.

I'm really happy that we're all friends again.

Since then I've tried to avoid fighting with the club. So even though I wasn't dying to win this D.J. contest, I figured I'd stick around.

"Really, Abby, have a little faith," Pamela was saying, elbow deep in mayo. "Besides, I thought you wanted to bring out your highlights so you'd look beautiful for Josh Baron tomorrow."

Josh Baron is a boy in our homeroom who Abby has a major crush on. We all think he likes her, too.

"I do," Abby muttered into the sink. "But I didn't think I was going to have to smell like a tuna fish sandwich."

"At least no one will think you're a breakfast cereal," Kate said, picking a large chunk of sticky granola from her long dark blonde curls. "Besides, I think Josh likes tuna fish sandwiches. I saw him eating one at lunch on Friday."

"Very funny, Kate," Abby said. "Pam! Ouch!"

"Beauty is well and good," Sarah said, careful to open her mouth only a little so the cucumbers stayed in place. "But poetry is the only true way to a man's heart."

"Does Lord Ivo say that?" I asked.

Lord Ivo is the hero in Sarah's favorite romance novels. She quotes him a lot.

"Regularly," Sarah replied. "Now, do you know what I think?"

She reached her long, skinny arm down to

5

scratch her knee, then licked the yogurt off her finger.

"Oh, Sarah, don't say it," Abby said.

Because we all knew exactly what Sarah thought. You see, she wants to be a writer when she grows up. She thinks poems are useful for any occasion.

"We should compose a poem for Josh," she said.

We all moaned.

"Okay, Sarah," said Kate from the floor. "How about 'When I look at Josh Baron, I can't keep from starin' . . .' "

Sarah thought for a minute, then shook her head.

"Hey, I've got one," I said. "'Josh, by gosh, I like you a losh.' "

But Sarah was serious.

"One ought never jest about matters of the heart," she said, piling her dark wavy hair on top of her head. "We need something lyrical. Romantic. An ode, perhaps."

Pam wasn't buying it.

"You guys sound like a bunch of dorfs," Pam said. "Boys couldn't care less about odes and stuff. All they care about is how you look."

She adjusted Sarah's cucumbers and plopped some more jelly into my hand lotion. "Which is exactly why we are beautifying."

This was the kind of thing Pam says sometimes that makes me feel absolutely lousy. I mean, just because she is so unbelievably gorgeous that she never has to worry about being smart or funny or talented or anything, doesn't mean that the rest of us don't. Geez, if boys only care about how you look, then I'll never get a boyfriend.

Suddenly I noticed that Pam was the only one of us not covered in goop. It just didn't seem fair, and I was getting bored sitting there. I pulled my hands out of Pam's softener, and a fingerful of grape and lemon glop shot out in her direction. It landed on her behind and stuck like glue.

"Oh, gee, sorry, Pam, that was an accident," I said, trying to keep from giggling.

"Way to go, Beth," Abby said.

I gave her a purple thumbs-up.

Pamela shook her head. "You may laugh now," she said, wrapping Abby's hair in a big, fluffy towel. "But you're all going to thank me tomorrow. Especially you two," she said to me and Abs. "So maybe you should try to be a little less obnoxious."

"It's hard, Pam," Abby said with a smile.

I nodded in agreement.

"Well, just remember, Abigail Wagner, that when Josh Baron says hi to you in English class tomorrow, it's because of me."

"Oh, of course, Pam," said Abby.

"And as for you, Miss I-want-the-lead-in-the-play-more-than-anything — " she said, turning to me.

"Yes, Pam," I interrupted her. "I'll know that I got to play Alice because of my beautiful, soft cuticles." I let fly another gob of her grape and lemon mixture, on purpose this time. It landed smack in the middle of her forehead. I burst out laughing.

"Bull's-eye," Kate said.

"Encore!" said Sarah.

Pam stood there for a minute with jelly dribbling down her face. Then she laughed, too, and held out her hands like she was going to choke me.

"Ooooh, I'm going to get you for this," said Pam, lurching toward me like she was Frankenstein.

I backed up, my gooey hands in the air, and hid behind the door.

"Here, Beth, let me help you," Kate called from the floor.

As Pam lurched over her, Kate smeared Pam's legs with honey and granola.

"HEELLPP!" cried Pam, trying to battle Kate's sticky hands. "Sarah, save me!"

"Fear not, fair Pamela. I'll bombard the enemy," Sarah said. Dripping yogurt all over the bathtub as she stood up, she began hurling cucumber slices at Kate and me.

"EEEEEKKKK!" I screamed as a cucumber slipped down my shirt.

"Let me at her. Let me at her," Abby said,

holding the half-empty jar of mayonnaise upside down over Pamela's head.

"Stop! Stop! Stop!" screamed Pam, but we were all laughing so hard, we could barely hear her.

Then, suddenly, we were quiet.

"Is that . . . ?" I asked.

"I think . . ." said Kate.

"TELEPHONE!" everyone shouted at once and, covered head to toe in food products, we raced out of the bathroom toward the kitchen. Pam took the lead.

"I want to answer it. You said I could answer it first," Kate whined, trying to weasel in front of me.

Sarah stepped back to let her pass.

"Go forth quickly, Kate," Sarah said. "WROK has little use for classical music lovers like myself."

With Kate gaining on the rest of us, we dashed through Pamela's huge gorgeous house, leaving sticky prints on everything we touched.

"Hurry!" Abby shouted. "Don't let Lucia get it."

Lucia was the Baldwins' housekeeper, and one of my favorite people to talk to. She always has incredibly interesting stories. The club thinks it's strange that I can sit in the kitchen listening to Lucia go on for hours about growing up in the South, or struggling to keep her family together, but they just don't have the patience I do. Personally, I think that it's absolutely necessary for an actress to try to understand as many different kinds of people as possible.

"Lucia!" we all called. "Don't answer the phone."

We rounded the corner to the kitchen and threw open the door. Lucia was standing next to the ringing phone, looking at us like we were from Mars.

"I got it," shrieked Pam.

"No, me. You said I could get the first call," Kate said again, grabbing the receiver out of Pam's hand.

"Don't worry," I said to Lucia, who was getting a good look at us all covered in muck. "We'll clean it up. How's your grandson feeling, by the way?" One of Lucia's thirteen grandsons had just broken his arm in a bicycle accident. I couldn't imagine having thirteen grandsons.

"SHHHHHH!" said Kate. She took a deep breath. The rest of us stood, dripping and quiet, with our fingers crossed.

"WROK — where you pick the hits," Kate said into the telephone.

We waited to see if Kate was going to start jumping up and down and screaming. But she just looked at us and shook her head. "Oh, hi, Mom," she said, rolling her eyes. "No, I don't normally answer the phone at the Baldwins.' We just thought it might be somebody else."

Oh, well.

"I knew it wouldn't be WROK," Abby said.

After about two hours, we'd managed to clean up most of our mess. We could probably have done it more quickly, but Kate was moping around after the phone call, and wasn't being much help. Her mom was going to be working late again that night, and had called to tell Kate to have dinner with one of us.

Kate's mom works all the time now, when she's not back in school. She got divorced recently, and she's trying to figure out a way to support Kate and her little sister Molly on her own. I like Mrs. Tucker a lot. She's very nice, and I think she'd feel bad if she knew how upset Kate gets when she calls like this. It really embarrasses Kate to always have to ask us if she can stay for meals or sleep over, or sometimes even borrow money. I think that sometimes she pretends to go home when nobody's there, just so it'll look like she's got a normal life. Once I saw her sitting all by herself outside the 7 Eleven, drinking an orange slush when she'd told me an hour before that she had to hurry home to meet her mom.

Anyway, I didn't want to eavesdrop on her conversation, but I could tell just by looking at her what her mom had said. So when she hung up the phone, I said, "Geez, Kate, I completely forgot. My mom told me to ask if you wanted to have

11

pizza with us tonight. We're going to Alfonso's. You interested?"

Kate pretended to think for a minute before answering.

"Sure, Beth, that sounds great," she said. And she punched me in the shoulder.

"Let me call my mom," I said. "To find out what time we're going."

I was really calling my mom to ask if Kate could join us, but I didn't say that. I knew that she knew, too, but this way, everybody felt better.

I had to let the phone ring at least a million times before my mom answered. She's the musical director of a local amateur theater group called the Small Town Players, and since she insists on playing her own piano, rehearsals have to be held at our house and it's hard to hear the phone ringing over all that noise. She would call it singing, but take it from me, it's noise. When she finally answered, she sounded a little hoarse, probably from shouting directions all afternoon, but she said it was no problem for Kate to come.

"What time is rehearsal going to be over?" I asked.

"You'll have to speak up, honey," Mom rasped. I could hear the actors in the background, botching up one of the songs from *Guys and Dolls*.

"WHAT TIME — " I started shouting, but Mom interrupted me.

"Beth, dear," she said. "I'm really right in the

middle of things here. Let me call you back when I can hear myself think." And she hung up the phone.

Sometimes it annoys me that my mom is so involved with a bunch of over-the-hill, would-be actors who take themselves very seriously. I suppose it might not bother me as much if I didn't want to be an actress so much myself. But I can't help worrying that instead of winning an Academy Award, I might wind up like them one day. Still, I know the group means a lot to my mom, who gets one hundred percent into whatever she's doing, even if it is only the dorfy Small Town Players. So I try not to let her know that I really think they're pretty awful.

I wandered back through Pam's house, and found the rest of the club in the living room, listening to music and dancing. Pam was standing on top of the coffee table and swinging her long golden hair around like she was one of those go-go dancers you see on old TV shows. Sometimes I can't help feeling plain when I look at her. I know that my mom says I'm pretty, and that I have nice hair and skin, but when I look in the mirror all I see is a round face, and gray-blue eyes that are a little too small, and absolutely no cheekbones at all. I wish that just once someone would stop me on the street to ask me if I was a model, or maybe a dancer.

Abby, Kate, and Sarah are all pretty, too, but

they're not drop-dead gorgeous like Pam is. Kate is tiny and skinny as a rail, and she has very curly blonde hair that always looks like it needs combing. Abby is medium height and medium weight, and her hair is medium length. She's got lots of freckles on her nose, and this really nice smile. As I said before, Sarah is the only one of us who's not blonde. She's got lots and lots of dark brown hair that gets frizzy in the rain. She's as tall and thin as Pamela, but for some reason it doesn't look as good on her. Pam looks like a model. Sarah looks like her pants are too short.

Anyway, Abby and Kate looked pretty funny trying to teach Sarah how to do some funky new dance steps. It seemed hopeless. It wasn't just that Sarah is so lanky and uncoordinated; there's something else about her that sets her apart from other kids our age. The way she talks. The books she reads. The music she listens to. It makes sense that she can't do the same dances we do. But I bet she could waltz perfectly at a ball.

Kate glanced over at me to see what the word was on dinner.

"Mom's calling back," I said, picking up the copy of *Alice in Wonderland* that I'd left on the TV. I opened the script to the Queen of Hearts scene and started thinking about the next day's auditions.

"I hope Mr. MacFadden will let me design some

of the scenery," Abby panted as she danced around in front of me.

"Oh, I'm sure he will," I said.

Abby's a wonderful artist. She wants to be a clothes designer when she grows up, and I know she'll be able to.

"Maybe he'll let me design your Alice costume," she said. "You'll look so cute in that little apron she always wears."

"Pinafore," Sarah corrected, stepping all over her own feet.

"And that blue dress with the puffy sleeves," Abby went on. "And your hair pulled back with a big white bow."

"Let's not get carried away, you guys," I said. "I don't have the part yet."

To be honest, I was surprised that she thought I'd look good in the Alice costume. I thought I might look sort of big and dorfy in it. It was my biggest worry about being in the play.

"Oh, please, Beth," said Pam from the coffee table. "Don't be so modest."

"Really," Kate said. "Who else would get the part?"

"You're the best actress in the whole school," said Abby.

"Gee, thanks," I said. It's great to have friends who believe in you. "Still, auditions are tomorrow. I have to do well."

"If you want," Kate said, "we can practice tonight after dinner. I'll read all the other parts."

Lucia came into the room, holding her hands over her ears to let us know that the music was too loud. Sometimes she can be just like a parent, which is probably a good thing since Pam's mom and dad work so hard that they are hardly ever home.

"I've got hot apple turnovers just out of the oven," she announced. "You girls want to come and help me eat them?"

"Yes, ma'am," Pam said.

"Well, maybe just one," I said.

"Come on, then," Lucia said, waving her arm at us. "I'll pour y'all some milk."

Five girls can eat an amazing number of hot apple turnovers. While we ate, Abby and Sarah told us about the latest chapter in the book they're writing. It's the story of the beautiful Annabella and her beloved Alexander, an Italian prince who was hiding from her evil uncle, the Marquis, and his cruel henchman, Pierre. Actually, Sarah's writing it, and Abby's doing the illustrations, which are absolutely gorgeous. In this chapter, Annabella had to pretend that she was in love with Pierre so that she could get into his private chambers and find the magic sapphire the Marquis had stolen from Alexander's mother.

"Poor Annabella," I said, listening to the story.

"She must be a great actress to be able to convince Pierre that she loves him."

"It is difficult for her," Sarah said. "But necessary. Certainly she cannot forfeit the magic sapphire."

"Look at this sketch for Annabella's nightgown," Abby said, pulling out a piece of paper and laying it in the turnover crumbs.

"Beautiful," we all agreed.

While we were discussing whether or not Annabella would let the cruel Pierre actually kiss her, the telephone rang. Sarah was sitting closest.

"It's my mom calling back about our dinner plans," I said. "Can you grab it, Sarah?"

Sarah stretched her long arm out for the phone.

"We'll probably meet everyone at my house and then head over to Alfonso's," I said to Kate, pushing back my chair so I could walk around to the phone.

Sarah put the receiver to her ear and gave us all a wink. "WROK — where you pick the hits," she said, laughing.

I put my hand out for Sarah to hand the phone over to me. Then I noticed that she had gotten up from the table. Her face was all red, and she was sort of rocking from foot to foot. "I beg your pardon?" she said. She looked absolutely surprised.

I glanced at the others. They were all watching

Sarah with their mouths slightly opened. I think we were all thinking the same thing.

"My name?" Sarah was saying. "Uh, Sarah. Sarah Stern."

"Do you think . . . ?" I said.

"Impossible," said Abby.

But Sarah was pointing to the phone and mouthing something that looked a lot like, "I won!" She had suddenly gotten very pale.

"I don't believe it," Pam said.

"I don't believe it, either," said Kate.

We all got up and stood in a little circle around Sarah. Finally, she hung up the phone. She looked like someone had just told her Lord Ivo had died. "You're not going to believe this," she said, falling into a chair. "I'm going to be a D.J."

2

It was pretty obvious from the way Sarah was acting that she thought winning the WROK contest was absolutely a catastrophe. She kept walking around the kitchen with her hand to her head, saying, "Woe is me. Woe is me." It turned out that she had never listened to WROK in her entire life. She'd never even *heard* of our favorite groups, The Rockets, Gordo Sax, and Moonrush. Pam was showing her how to speak in that fast, loud D.J. kind of style when my mom actually did call to tell us to head on home. As Kate and I left, Sarah was repeating after Pam, "WROK is your radio station." I know she was trying, but somehow she just sounded like a librarian.

Pam, Kate, and I live on the same street, and I always walk home from the Baldwins' house exactly the same way. First, I go past the big ivy-covered house that Abby and her family used to live in, before they moved to a house across the street from Sarah on Big Bottom Road. Then I walk by the huge linden tree where some of the high school kids carve their initials inside of hearts. From there I cross to the other side and try to balance along the crumbly stone wall that the Not For Blondes Only club used to pretend was a castle, and finally by old Miss Frost's big blue Victorian house.

Miss Frost turned ninety-three on her last birthday. She never got married, and has lived in the same house on Honey Hollow Road since she was just a little girl. The club thinks Miss Frost is a little bit creepy, probably because she's so ancient, but I love to listen to her stories about the olden days when she'd ride in horse-drawn carriages, and Honey Hollow Road was nothing but dirt and fields. She was sitting on her front porch wrapped up in a blanket when Kate and I walked by.

"Hello, Miss Frost." I waved to her.

Kate waved, too, but only because it would be impolite not to.

"Oh, hello, Elizabeth, dear," said Miss Frost, squinting through her funny round glasses to see me better. "Isn't it a lovely day?"

"How are you feeling?" I asked. I spoke much louder than usual because Miss Frost is hard of hearing.

"Full of spit and vinegar," said Miss Frost.

I smiled. Miss Frost knew a lot of old sayings like that.

"There's a new litter of puppies out back," Miss Frost went on. "Come up and see them, and please bring all your little blonde friends."

Miss Frost used to have lots of dogs. Sometimes she forgets that she doesn't have them anymore.

"Some other time," I said. Kate was pulling at my sleeve. "My mom's waiting for us."

"Good-bye, dear," she said.

"Geez, I hope I never get that old," said Kate as we crossed back over toward my house.

"I hope I get even older," I said. "Think about all the stuff you'd know."

Our driveway was still packed with cars, which meant that Mom's rehearsal wasn't over yet. That didn't surprise me. Mom always gets carried away when she's working and forgets about the time. She also forgets about going to the grocery store, doing the laundry — *everything*, actually. She says it's hard for her to concentrate on more than one thing at a time. Rather than interrupt her, Kate and I went around the back and in through the kitchen door.

My dad was sitting at the table reading a medical journal. He's an obstetrician, which is the kind of doctor that delivers babies. In front of him was a cup of coffee, his beeper from the hospital, and a bag of pastel-colored cotton balls. From the living room I could hear one of the Small Town Players croaking out a song.

"Hiya, Daddy," I said loudly.

"Hi, Dr. Hanson," shouted Kate.

When he didn't answer, Kate and I looked at each other and smiled. Then I walked over and kissed him on his bald spot. Dad looked up with a start, and grinned when he saw us.

"Well, well, well, how're my girls?" he asked, putting down his journal.

I gave him the okay sign. "Rehearsal's not over yet?" I shouted.

Dad shook his head. I could see a blue cotton ball stuffed in each ear. "Been brutal here today," he said. "Think they're getting worse with each rehearsal. Don't know how Mom can stand it. Here, catch."

Dad tossed me the bag of cotton balls. I pulled out a couple, handed the bag to Kate, and we stuffed them in our ears. Poor Dad. He looked even more tired than usual. For some reason, women always seem to have their babies between midnight and three in the morning, and the night before, one of his patients had triplets. When my dad gets tired, his eyes sort of sink into his face, and his cheeks droop. He looks just like one of those basset hound dogs, only with a mustache. I reached out and patted him on the hand. "Anything to eat?" I yelled.

Dad shook his head sadly.

"*Guys and Dolls* diet," he said with a sigh. "Mom promises she'll go to the grocery store tomorrow."

We have a joke in our house that we always lose weight when mom works on a new show. Last spring we all went on the *Chorus Line* diet. I suppose if she worked with the Small Town Players for the rest of her life, I'd eventually wind up thin.

"Where's Alison?" I asked.

Dad pointed in the direction of the living room and shrugged. For some reason, my nine-and-a-half-year-old sister enjoys these rehearsals. She can sit in the living room for hours, no cotton balls at all, and actually have a good time.

Then Dad patted his stomach. "I'm starving," he bellowed. "Stick your nose in there on your way upstairs to let Mom know you're home."

Kate and I poured ourselves the last of the grape juice and, arranging our hair over our ears so that no one would notice the cotton balls, stepped into the living room. Mom was sitting at the piano, running her hand through her short brown hair, while two of her actors were ruining a song.

"Hiya, Mom," I called to her.

"Hi, Mrs. Hanson," called Kate.

My mom winked in our direction, glanced at her watch, and held her index finger in the air to mean "just a minute." Then she turned back to her actors.

Even though the Small Town Players absolutely stink, I love watching my mom in rehearsal, bang-ing away at the piano and mouthing all the words. Mom is a wonderful musician. She plays piano and clarinet and has a beautiful voice. When I was little, she used to sing me to sleep every single night, lying next to me all snuggled up in bed. Even now, if I'm feeling particularly sad or silly, she'll crawl under the covers with me and we'll sing together. She may not be the most organized person in the world, but as moms go, I am very lucky.

From a corner of the room, Alison came bounding toward us, chomping on a piece of bubble gum.

"Hi, you guys," she said, letting a big bubble pop right in our faces. "Great rehearsal today." She reached toward me and pulled my hair. "Naughty, naughty," she said obnoxiously, looking at my ears. "Cotton balls. I'm going to tell."

"Shhhhh," I said, making sure Mom didn't hear her. Not that she doesn't know about the cotton ball trick. But I think it hurts her feelings a little. "Geez, Alison. Do you think you could maybe be normal for once?"

I don't know how it happened, but Alison is absolutely a brat. I'm sure that Mom and Dad did their best with her. I just think it's in her blood. Luckily, since Kate has a younger sister, too, she understands.

"You know, you've got some kind of junk on your face," Alison said to Kate, leaning in to take a closer look. "What is that, cereal?"

"If you must know," Kate said evenly, "I applied a honey-and-granola mask this afternoon." She brushed some remaining cereal crumbs off her cheek.

"A beauty treatment," I added.

"Oh," said Alison, skipping back to her corner. "It didn't work."

I took a deep breath to keep from punching her.

"Your sister . . ." muttered Kate as we headed upstairs to my room.

"Don't I know it," I agreed. "Let's spike her soda at Alfonso's."

As usual, it took over an hour for us to actually leave for dinner. First, Mom couldn't find her purse. Then the hospital beeped my dad to say that one of his patients had gone into labor. Then Mom couldn't find her keys. Then the dishwasher started to sputter, and Mom remembered that she'd forgotten to call the plumber. Then Dad's beeper beeped again. I'm used to this kind of commotion, but I felt kind of bad for Kate. It's hard enough to be shipped off to another family without the other family being a bunch of nuts. Finally, we all piled into the car to rush to the restaurant so that Dad could have a couple of slices before dashing off to the hospital again.

We couldn't find parking anywhere near Alfonso's, so we had to leave the car about three blocks away. On our walk back to the restaurant, we passed a pay phone and Dad decided to call the hospital to see how his patient was doing. Usually it takes a pretty long time to have a baby, so he doesn't need to get there right away.

I think my dad is a great doctor. There's something calm and strong about him, plus he can always make you laugh even when you don't feel like it. And from what I hear, you don't exactly feel like laughing when you're having a baby. But sometimes I feel bad that he always has to get up in the middle of things to go and take care of somebody else. When I was younger and he'd miss a school play or a recital, I'd feel really hurt. But, now, mostly I think that if he wasn't already my dad, I'd wish he was.

While he was on the phone, Kate, Mom, and Alison looked in the different shops, while I waited on a bench on the curb. I hate shopping. It's my least favorite thing. Nothing ever fits, or if it does fit, it's the wrong color, or if it's the right color, then it's too expensive so you can't get it anyway. The mirrors make you look worse than you already do, the salesgirls always tell you how absolutely excellent you look in stuff that makes you want to barf, and your mom can't stand the one cool outfit that you finally bring home. Some people seem to have more of a knack for it than I do. Pamela, for one, is an expert shopper. But I'm better off just sitting on a bench and saving myself the aggravation.

It was a nice night, anyway, and lots of people

were walking up and down the street. I have this game that I play, in which I choose someone out of the crowd and then try to imagine how that person talks, where that person works, that kind of thing. It's a really fun game, plus I think it'll help me in my acting career. I was hoping that someone particularly interesting or weird would stroll by when I noticed two people kissing in a doorway. The guy was really tall, and the girl had beautiful, black hair that was tumbling all over her shoulders and, well, I know this sounds absolutely dorfy, but they just looked really romantic standing there.

Personally, I don't know much about kissing. I've never been kissed by a boy in my entire life. Not even once. I almost got to kiss Marco Hernandez when I was in the seventh-grade musical, but that didn't even work out. Pamela was kissed a couple of times by a boy she met at camp, but not on the lips. She said it was no big thrill, but I don't believe her. I just hope that someone will want to kiss me someday. I'm dying to know what it feels like.

Sarah says that Lord Ivo goes around kissing people all over the place, and that every girl he kisses falls in love with him. That makes sense to me. It would be pretty gross to be kissing someone who you weren't in love with, considering how close you have to be to that person to do it. I mean, they could have bad breath or a zit or a runny nose. But if you were in love with them, you probably wouldn't even notice.

I wish I could figure out how you learn how to do it. It's not as if they teach it at school or anything, and it would be beyond embarrassing to ask your mom or dad. But what if I actually found someone who wanted to kiss me and I didn't know how? Pamela says it comes naturally. She might be right about short kisses, but I worry that when it comes to the long ones, I won't know when to breathe. I guess it's just something you learn as you get older, the way you learn to like artichoke hearts.

The two people in the doorway looked like pretty experienced kissers. They were doing the long kind and seemed to be breathing absolutely fine. I watched the way the girl was drooped over the guy's arm so he sort of had to hold her up. It looked like they were dancing.

Kate, Mom, and Alison had finished browsing and were waiting to see what was up with my dad. Alison was sort of dangling from the phone booth making choking noises, pretending to be dying of hunger. Mom was hunting through her purse to see if she'd remembered to bring her wallet. I walked over to see something Kate wanted to show me in a window.

"I love that shirt," she said, pointing at a skimpy little midriff thing that only tiny skinny girls like Kate could wear.

"Pretty," I said. I was still looking at the kissers. I couldn't believe the way they were going at it. I figured one of them must be going away, or dying of some deadly disease or something. I hoped it wasn't catching. I could see them better from this angle because of the lights from the store window, and I was amazed how much the guy looked like Mr. MacFadden.

Now, Mr. MacFadden was someone I could definitely kiss.

I gave Kate a nudge. "Isn't it weird how that guy looks like Mr. MacFadden?" I said.

"Uh-huh," Kate answered without really looking. She was too busy thinking about the shirt in the window. But then she did a double take, just like in the movies, and this time her mouth dropped open.

"Beth," she hissed. "It *is* Mr. MacFadden."

"You're nuts," I said, taking another look. By now they had stopped kissing and were just sort of snuggling together. I could get a better view of the girl. She had perfect cheekbones and huge brown eyes. Then she said something that made the guy laugh, and he lifted his head.

"OH, MY GOSH!" I said, pulling Kate away from the window before Mr. MacFadden saw us. "OH, MY GOSH! OH, MY GOSH!"

We ran over to the phone booth, where my dad had finally finished talking, and ducked behind my mother. Then, from between the folds of Mom's coat, we took another peek at Mr. MacFadden. I couldn't believe it. They were at it again. Mr. MacFadden must be the greatest kisser in the entire world. This is not the kind of thing you're supposed to know about your English teacher.

"Girls, what is going on?" Mom asked, yanking the hem of her coat out of our hands.

I put my finger to my lips so Kate wouldn't say anything.

"Oh, nothing, Mom," I said. "Let's just go eat."

I knew if I told my mom that Mr. MacFadden was over there, she'd make me say hello. She always makes a point of meeting my teachers. She thinks it's rude not to. One time we saw Ms. Feingold, my fifth-grade teacher, at a friend's country club, and Mom actually invited her to join us for lunch. I had to smile a lot and pretend that I remembered the stuff she'd taught me, and the worst thing about it was that Ms. Feingold was wearing this tiny pink bikini and kept getting bread crumbs all over her chest. It was absolutely the pits. I knew that if I told Mom that Mr. MacFadden was over there, kissing for the world's record, she'd make me walk right over and tap him on the shoulder. That's the kind of thing Mom thinks is polite.

Fortunately, she was really hungry, so she gave us a look that meant "stop being silly," and we all headed toward Alfonso's. Unfortunately, Alison recognized Mr. MacFadden.

He had finally stopped kissing the girl, and they were strolling hand in hand, talking and laughing. Kate and I were practically walking in the traffic, we were trying so hard to avoid them. We would have been home free if Alison hadn't opened her mouth. She must have some kind of little sister ESP, because if there's something she can do to embarrass me, she'll immediately figure out what it is and do it. Anyway, I knew we were sunk when I heard her call out in her phony, grown-up voice, "Why, hello, Mr. MacFadden."

Needless to say, Mom jumped right in. "Why, Mr. MacFadden, how nice to see you. Beth has been talking about the play all week. She's so excited. Do you know my husband, Mark?"

And so there we were. My dad was saying hello to Mr. MacFadden, and being introduced to Victoria, his girlfriend. Alison was sticking out her tongue at me behind Mom's back. Mr. MacFadden was laughing and rubbing his girlfriend on the neck. And everyone was acting as if this were the most normal thing in the whole world. Except me and Kate. We were shuffling our feet, hoping that after all the adult politeness was over with, Mr. MacFadden and his girlfriend would just keep on walking. No such luck.

"I must say, you two are unusually quiet tonight," Mr. MacFadden said, looking right at us. I couldn't believe he could talk to us while he was rubbing his girlfriend's neck like that. Especially after all that kissing. Of course, he didn't know we saw the kissing, but still. It made me really nervous. And when I'm nervous like that, I always do the same thing. I start to giggle. Kate starts to giggle, too.

"There you go. That's more like the Beth and Kate I know," said Mr. MacFadden. Then he turned to his girlfriend. "These two gigglers are some of my very best students."

"Well, I hope Willie's not too tough on you," said his girlfriend.

WILLIE! I thought I would die right on the spot. I kept biting the inside of my mouth to keep from completely losing it. Kate looked like she was ready to pee in her pants. Mom was glaring at me. I know she thought that we were absolutely rude. But Mr. MacFadden didn't seem to notice.

"Oh, I'm an ogre, aren't I, girls?" he said. But he said it more to his girlfriend than he did to us. She seemed to think it was the funniest thing in the world.

"Ha, ha, ha, ha," laughed his girlfriend. And she gave him a hug.

"Well, we'd better be pushing off," Mr. MacFadden finally said. "I'll see you in auditions tomorrow, right, Beth?"

I managed to nod.

"You too, Kate," Mr. MacFadden said as he started to leave. "I'm counting on you, okay?" Then he winked at us, put his arm around his girlfriend's shoulder, and headed down the street.

I don't really remember the rest of the evening. Mom said something about our childish behavior, and Alison said something about how beautiful Victoria was, and my dad had to leave for the hospital before his pizza was even served. Kate was worried about going to the audition because she'd never done any acting before, but I told her that I couldn't possibly face Mr. MacFadden by myself. Besides, there are a lot of small parts in *Alice in Wonderland* that I thought might be fun for her.

It was hard for me to fall asleep that night. I kept picturing Mr. MacFadden over and over in my mind, kissing Victoria in the doorway. Then I had a dream that I had won the Academy Award for kissing, and that Mr. MacFadden was going to present it to me. But just as I reached the stage, Alison woke me up on her way to the bathroom, so I'll never know how it ended.

3

"*W*illie?" Pam said, not believing me.

"Willie," I said.

I was sitting with the Not For Blondes Only club at lunch the next day. Sarah isn't in our homeroom, so Kate and I had to wait until lunch when we could all sit together to tell them about Mr. MacFadden. Kate was letting me tell the story because I'm better at it than she is. I have to admit I am pretty good at telling a story. I'm not like Sarah, who absolutely makes them up out of her head, but I can tell a story about something I saw or did. Sometimes when something particularly interesting happens — like seeing Mr. MacFadden kissing his girlfriend on the street — part of me is already thinking about how I'll tell the club about it afterwards. Last year when my parents took us camping in the woods, and it rained for three days, and Alison got poison ivy, and Mom forgot the maps, and then the car got a flat tire, the only thing that kept me going was

34

thinking about what a great story it would make. And I have to admit that the club laughed about it for days, particularly the part about Alison having poison ivy on her behind. The Mr. MacFadden story was also a big hit.

"That's utterly romantic," Sarah sighed. "I think it must be splendid to be so in love."

"Well, I think it's gross," Pam said.

"Why?" Abby asked.

"It's just gross to think about a teacher kissing like that. It gives me the creeps," Pam replied.

"That's ridiculous, Pam. Teachers are people, too. They can fall in love just like anyone else," Abby said. "Especially *Willie*." We all started laughing again. "I think he's very romantic."

"Indeed," said Sarah.

Sarah and Abby also have a little crush on Mr. MacFadden. Sarah even wrote a whole story about him once for Ellen Wu and Peggy Phillips, these two girls in our class. Ellen and Peggy are absolutely in *love* with Mr. MacFadden.

"I just don't know how we're going to face him at auditions," Kate said.

"Auditions?" said Pam. "I thought we were all going to the mall with Sarah to pick out clothes."

It was sort of funny the way Pam was taking Sarah under her wing and teaching her how to be a rock-and-roll D.J. and shopping with her, when just a little while ago she hated Sarah's guts and was never going to talk to Abby again for being

35

friends with her. My mom says that they didn't get along at first because they both have such strong personalities. They're still sort of an odd couple, and this was the first time they ever did anything just the two of them. But I was glad they were getting along so well because I really like Sarah, and I know that it means a lot to Abby that we changed the club to *Not* For Blondes Only, and made her a member. It's been nice for the club, too.

"Kate can't come to the mall with you, Pam. She promised to go to auditions with me," I said. "I just can't face *Willie* all by myself."

"Well, I guess it will be sort of hard to keep from puking when you see him," Pam said. "Abby and I will have to do Sarah's make-over ourselves. I've been looking in *Teen Girl* magazine for ideas, and I think I've found the perfect thing for all that hair of hers — "

"Well, actually, Pam, I'm thinking of auditioning, too," Abby slipped in very casually.

"What?" Pam said. "Abby, I need you! Anyway, you hate getting up in front of people. I thought you were just going to do scenery or something."

"Well, I thought it might be interesting to try out, that's all," Abby said. "Anyway, I don't know why Sarah has to change her hair just to be on the radio. It's not like anyone's going to see her."

"'If you look good, you feel good' — that's what my mother always says," Pam replied. "Since when are you interested in acting, anyway?"

"Since she found out that Josh Baron was auditioning," Kate said. "I overheard him telling Charlie Goldstein this morning."

"OOOOOOOOOOOOOOHHHHHHHH," we all said together.

It's interesting that Abby is the first member of the club to have a boy who likes her at our school. Not that she isn't cute and funny and smart. It's just that Pam is so gorgeous, you would think all the boys would go for her. Sometimes I think boys might find Pam a little scary, though, because she's kind of snotty to them. Anyway, I was glad it was Abby. Not just because she's such a great friend, but also because she wouldn't lord it over anyone that she had a boy who liked her. I think sometimes she's actually kind of embarrassed about it.

"Shut up, you guys!" she whispered, turning about ten shades of red.

"Well, I would never stand in the way of true love," Pam said.

"Nor I!" added Sarah. "Certainly a romantic attachment is of far more import than my lack of chic. Oh, Abby, perhaps you will perform together."

"Maybe you'll have to kiss him!" Kate teased. "I bet *Willie* could give him really expert advice."

"There's no kissing in *Alice in Wonderland*, Kate," Abby mumbled, sort of between her teeth.

"It would be great if we all got parts, wouldn't it?" I said, changing the subject. I hate it when anyone starts to feel humiliated, particularly Abby, because she gets embarrassed easily.

"Yes, I think it would be quite thrilling," said Sarah. "Even *I* sometimes think about the smell of the greasepaint . . . coming onstage to the sounds of *'Bravo, bravissimo,'* the roaring thunder of the applause as you proudly take your bow — "

"Well, you're not taking any bows this time, Sarah," Pam interrupted. "We have shopping to do, and then we're going to my house and teaching you how to talk like a normal person, and then we're going to listen to every tape I own until you know the WROK Top-Twenty by heart. And if none of you will help me, I'll do it myself. It's been done before."

"Just like Henry Higgins and Eliza Doolittle in *My Fair Lady,*" I said.

"Actually, I was thinking about that episode in *The Brady Bunch* where Marsha turns a dorfball into the most popular girl at school," Pam said. "What's *My Fair Lady?*"

My Fair Lady is my all-time favorite musical. My mom did it with the Small Town Players two years ago. All the songs in it are just beautiful, but there sure are a lot of them. My dad always says that the *My Fair Lady* diet worked better than Weight Watchers. I think we all lost about five pounds. I loved the show, though. I even asked for the videotape of the movie for my birthday last year. Sarah and Abby watch it with me all the time, because it's absolutely Sarah's kind of movie. It's about how Henry Higgins teaches Eliza Doolittle, the poor little cockney girl, to speak proper English, and dress and act like a lady. Then she goes to the Embassy ball and everyone thinks she's a Hungarian princess.

"I like when she goes to the ball," Kate said.

"No, I like the part when she sings about the rain in Spain," Abby replied.

"All right, so what is it?" Pam asked.

"Oh, I feel quite inspired, now," Sarah said. "I assure you, Pam, that I will do my best to emulate Eliza Doolittle, and transform myself."

"What are you all talking about?!" Pam said. She hates it when she's left out.

So for the rest of lunch, we all told her the story of *My Fair Lady*. We even sang the songs, until Abby saw Josh Baron looking at us funny and made us stop.

"Now that's real music," Sarah said. "Perhaps I could play some of that on the radio."

"I can tell we've got a lot of work ahead of us." Pam sighed.

After lunch I had to go to math class, but I had a really hard time concentrating, I was so worried about the auditions. It's hard to think about common denominators when you have a hive of butterflies inside you. Sometimes I think I'm crazy to want to be an actress so much. I'm always so nervous before auditions that my palms start to sweat, and I get sick to my stomach.

After class, Abby and Kate and I walked together to Mr. MacFadden's homeroom. He was sitting at his desk in front of the classroom, and he had turned all the other desks around so that they formed a big circle. Mr. MacFadden looked just the way he always did, in his brown corduroy jacket with the patches on the sleeves. It was hard to believe that only last night he had been passionately kissing someone right in front of me. If Kate hadn't been there with me, I would have thought it was just a dream.

Ellen Wu and Peggy Phillips were there, which wasn't at all surprising. I knew they would try out for any play if Mr. MacFadden was involved in it. They were already giggling together like crazy. They giggle more than any other girls in the whole school. If they had seen Mr. MacFadden kissing a beautiful girl in the middle of Elm Street, they probably would have giggled themselves to death. Charlie Goldstein and Josh Baron were there, too.

"Hi, Abs," Josh called.

"Hi," Abby replied, getting very red.

That was all they said. Then Abby and Kate

and I sat down about as far away from the boys as possible. Compared to Mr. MacFadden's love life, I have to say that ours are pretty boring.

After a while, six or seven more kids came into the room, and Mr. MacFadden decided to start. The butterflies in my stomach were getting worse and worse. First he handed around a piece of paper so every one of us could sign our names. He also asked us to write down any backstage work we might be interested in.

I knew Abby was going to sign up to do scenery, but I didn't want to do anything if I didn't get a part. I didn't think I could stand it to sit through all the rehearsals and the play and everything and not be on stage. I thought it would just be depressing. But I've always gotten a part in our class play since I was a really little kid and played the tooth with the cavity. That was in the third grade, and the show was called *Brush and Floss*. Kate was a molar. Abby and Pam were in a different homeroom, and they did a play about litter.

Then Mr. MacFadden handed out copies of the script and started to have people read scenes. First he had Ellen Wu read the part of Alice. She was not very good. I don't like to say anything mean about anyone, but she giggled every other word, plus she kept getting the lines mixed up and reading the Cheshire Cat's lines by mistake. Charlie Goldstein was reading the Cheshire Cat, and he *was* good. I wasn't surprised, though, because he's the smartest boy in the whole class, and he's good at everything.

Anyway, after hearing Ellen Wu, I wasn't as worried. I knew I'd do much better than her. So when Mr. MacFadden asked me to read, I was calm. All the butterflies in my stomach had flown away, and I was absolutely ready. I was sure I would get the part of Alice. There was a little voice inside me that just knew.

Which goes to show you how much you can believe those little voices inside you. Mr. MacFadden asked me to read six times! Once for the Queen of Hearts, twice for the March Hare, and twice for Tweedledee. And once for Alice. *Once.* Abby read three times. And Kate? Kate read five times for Alice. Five times. By the end of auditions, I wanted to cry. I knew if he had let me read a few more times, I could have shown him how well I could do it. But it was pretty obvious that he just wasn't going to let me. I never had a chance! It wasn't fair.

By the time auditions were over and we were all walking home together, I was so depressed I could hardly stand it.

Kate sure didn't feel that way, though. She was so excited, she was hopping down the school steps. "That was so much fun!" Kate exclaimed. "Beth, I'm so glad you made me go."

"You were great, Kate!" Abby said. "I didn't know you could act."

"Neither did I," Kate replied. "Do you think I'll get a part?"

Little Miss Innocent. As if she didn't know she was probably going to get the starring role. The thing that killed me was I absolutely couldn't blame Mr. MacFadden. Looking at Kate, I could see why he would want her to play Alice in Wonderland. She looks like Alice in Wonderland. She is so cute and perky, and she has long, pretty hair. She'd look great in that pinafore thing. I probably couldn't even fit down the rabbit hole.

"You were great, too, Beth," Abby said. "When you read for the Queen of Hearts, I really got scared."

"Yeah," I said. Yes, that was me all right. The Queen of Hearts. The big, mean, ugly Queen of Hearts. Yuck.

"I know something you don't know," Kate sang out, nudging Abby.

"What?" Abby asked.

"I saw the sign-up sheet on Mr. MacFadden's desk after auditions, and guess who signed up to do scenery with you!"

"Really?" Abby said.

"Yes!" Kate said. "Isn't that neat?"

I figured they must mean Josh Baron.

"Neat," I said.

43

Great. Now Abby was hopping up and down the stairs. This was all I needed. There's nothing worse than feeling miserable when everyone you know is feeling terrific.

"I bet he saw your name and signed up just so he could be with you," Kate gushed. "I think that's so romantic."

"Yeah," I said. "Maybe you can actually have a real conversation one day, too."

"Beth!" Kate said.

"Well, gee, Kate, all they ever say to each other is 'hi.' It's not much of a romance if you can't even get past that," I said.

Right away I felt bad that I'd said it. It wasn't Abby's fault that she didn't know what to say to a boy. I didn't know what to say to a boy. And it wasn't her fault that Kate was probably going to get the lead in the class play, and I was going to get some stupid part like the Queen of Hearts. But even though I felt bad that I'd said it, I didn't want to take it back, either. I had this big lump in the bottom of my stomach, and it made me feel really mean. Suddenly, instead of hating to fight, I sort of wanted to.

"Well, when you're working together back-stage, you'll have lots of things to talk about," Kate said to Abby.

"Yeah," I added, "you can say, 'please pass the red paint.' "

That sounded kind of mean, too, I guess, but I

44

couldn't help myself. And just as I said it, I looked up and there was Josh Baron himself, walking down the school steps. Abby was in mid-hop when she saw him, and she was so surprised that she slipped and fell right down on her behind. And that was when I did the absolutely meanest thing of the whole afternoon. I laughed. Not a lot, and not really loud or anything, but enough for her to notice. Abby turned positively purple with embarrassment. But then Josh came running down the rest of the stairs.

"Are you okay?" he asked, sounding really worried.

"Yeah, fine, just fine," Abby said, but you could tell by the way she was getting up that she was hurt a little bit.

As he was helping her stand up, she stumbled again a little, and he caught her so that his arm was around her waist for about one second. It was an absolutely intense moment. Kate and I stood there watching with our mouths hanging open. Abby and Josh looked right into each other's eyes, just like at the movies. Then Abby turned even purpler than ever, and Josh sort of coughed, and they were back to normal.

"Thanks," Abby said.

"Welcome," Josh replied.

"So."

"Yeah."

"Well."

"Well."

"Thanks again."

"Bye."

"Bye." Josh waved and took off like a shot. It was probably the longest conversation they'd ever had. It made me more depressed than ever. I just couldn't believe the way the week was turning out. First Sarah wins the radio contest, then Kate is the star of the *Alice in Wonderland* auditions, and to top it all off, everyone and their English teacher is falling in love right in front of me. It was getting awfully depressing.

"Oh, Abby," Kate sighed. "He came running to your rescue. Hasn't this just been the greatest day?"

Great for you two, I thought.

"Yeah," Abby said.

"It's a good thing you're so clumsy, Abs," I said. "You should fall down like that more often." Well, that was it. I couldn't *stop* the nasty things from coming out of my mouth. "Ha-ha. Just kidding," I added quickly.

I began to wonder. Pamela can sometimes be so nasty, you want to stuff a sock in her mouth. Maybe that's because she's feeling as lousy as I was. Maybe sometimes she feels that life is unfair, too, and that's why she says those things. Although life has been more than fair to Pamela, if you ask me. So I don't know. All I do know is that I couldn't hang around with Kate and Abby anymore. I didn't want to hear about Josh Baron, or about how great the auditions were, or about anything. Plus, I knew I was going to say something unforgivable if I didn't watch out.

"Well, I have to get going," I said. "I've got a ton of homework, and I told my mom I'd stop at Deli Delicious on my way home and get some milk."

"Okay," said Kate.

"Okay," Abby said, still in a kind of a daze from actually touching Josh Baron.

"I'll see you later," I said.

I walked down the rest of the steps and turned the corner as fast as I could. The big lump of meanness in the bottom of my stomach was moving right up into my throat, and the last thing I wanted was for anyone to see me cry.

4

I didn't really have to pick up anything at Deli Delicious. I just wanted to see one of the guys there, Vinnie, who owns the place. Vinnie's one of those people who always has bad luck. Last week his car was stolen. The week before, the electric company turned off his lights. Twice in one month he locked himself out of his house and had to climb in through the attic window. And for Vinnie, who's about fifty years old and is shaped like a meatball, that's not so easy.

I like to go see Vinnie whenever I'm feeling down. He's a good listener, and he's almost always got a worse problem himself. And, sometimes, hearing about other people's problems makes me feel a little better about my own. It makes me feel less alone, more like we're all in this mess together. I know Miss Frost has a saying about that, but I can't remember it.

The other thing about Vinnie is that if I did start to cry, which was becoming more and more likely with every step I took, he wouldn't think it was stupid or anything. He's a very emotional guy himself. I've seen him cry lots of times, particularly when they play this one Italian song on the radio that reminds him of his father. After a good cry, he likes to eat hot peppers and sliced pepperoni. Vinnie's one of those people in my life who the Not For Blondes Only club doesn't understand at all, but I'm glad he's my friend.

The red and white awning of the deli was up ahead, and I was getting ready to let the tears just come when I heard someone calling my name. Pamela and Sarah were running toward me from across the street. Pam had shopping bags in each hand, and the flushed, happy look she gets after a successful day at the mall.

"Hurray! Beth! Just the person we wanted to see," Pam bubbled. "We've been shop-shop-shopping for Sarah's new look. Now we're going back to my house to put it all together. You coming?"

"Well, uh . . ." I wasn't really in the mood for company, particularly if I was going to have to talk about auditions. And I was nervous that the lump of meanness had not completely gone away. I didn't want to be mean to Sarah. And I definitely didn't want to be mean to Pam. She can be very mean back. "I don't know. I sort of had stuff to do and, well . . ."

"Please, Beth," Sarah pleaded. "I could use a

little moral support before undergoing such a major transformation." She looked nervously at the shopping bags in Pam's hands.

I pictured Sarah strapped to a table, while Pam, wearing a white lab coat and cackling madly, mixed weird steaming chemicals in big glass test tubes.

"Please," Sarah said again.

Pam was waiting with one hand on her hip, tapping her foot. What am I worried about? I thought to myself. They're both so involved in this WROK thing, they won't even remember we had auditions today. Usually I don't like it when people are so self-involved, but this time, it was perfect. I looked deep into my stomach, and it was lump-free.

"All right," I agreed.

"Great," said Sarah, sounding relieved.

"Let's go then," said Pam. "We have lots of work to do."

The first thing Pam did when we got back to her house was empty all the shopping bags, and the entire contents of her own closet, onto her bed. I couldn't believe all the stuff. There were combs and ponytail holders and hair spray and mousse. There were eye pencils and lipsticks and nail polish in weird colors. There were tank tops and tube skirts, earrings, woven bracelets, and crystals. And not a single solitary thing looked like anything I could ever picture Sarah wearing in a million, quadrillion years.

Clearly, Sarah felt the same way.

"I have grave misgivings about this whole plan," she said staring at herself in the mirror.

"Oh, stop it," Pam said, gathering armfuls of wild outfits from the bed. "This is going to be fun!"

"But I'm not designed to be cool," Sarah continued. "It's not in my genes. I will disgrace myself and bring shame upon my family."

I looked at Sarah standing there in her T-shirt and underpants in front of Pam's full-length mirror. She was so tall and skinny, all arms, legs, and big feet, with an enormous head of dark curls. Sarah was right. Cool was not her middle name. Still, Pam could work miracles. And what about Eliza Doolittle in *My Fair Lady*? Then I had a brainstorm.

"You know, Sarah," I said. "Maybe you should think of it as a disguise. Lord Ivo is always doing stuff in disguise, isn't he?"

"Indeed," Sarah said.

"Well, if he can do it, so can you. Just pretend that you're, I don't know, a princess or something." I wasn't very good at this Lord Ivo thing, but that was okay. Sarah was great at it.

"Oh, yes," she said, lighting up. "And a villainous conjurer, determined to overtake my throne, has forced me into a time machine, leaving me stranded at a twentieth-century radio station."

"Exactly," I said. It was amazing how Sarah could come up with this stuff off the top of her head.

"And so now, I must shed the trappings of my former life and, with the help of Pamela, a beautiful and kindhearted fashion model, blend in with the common folk, all the while awaiting my rescue."

"There you go," I said. Cheering Sarah up like that had made me feel better. I was barely thinking about auditions at all anymore.

"Well, then," said Sarah, standing straighter and taller and more like a princess. "Pamela, you may begin."

"Okeydokey," said Pam. "Let's do it, Your Highness."

For the next forty-five minutes, Pam primped and poked and squeezed and squished and teased and tossed Sarah into more outfits and hairstyles than I could even imagine. She tried on leopard-print leotards and orange tube dresses, polka-dot leggings and flowered miniskirts. She used red lipstick and black lipstick, fake fingernails and fake eyelashes. It was like watching one of those scenes in a movie where they want to show how the guy and the girl are falling in love. First they're playing hopscotch with a bunch of little kids. Then the girl is trying on a lot of silly hats while the guy takes pictures and, finally, you see them in a rowboat at sunset. A montage, Pam calls it. Anyway, I felt like I was watching a montage of Sarah, except that instead of having sappy soundtrack music in the background, we were listening to Pam's tape collection so that Sarah could learn the different tunes.

"She's my high-heeled honey, and I love the way she steps on me," Pam and I sang along. Sarah, dressed in a black tube skirt and oversized black T-shirt, her dark brown hair moussed so much that her bangs stood straight up in the air, was studying her reflection.

"Okay, Sarah, I mean, Your Highness, do you know what group this is?" Pam asked, hanging a huge crystal on a leather cord around Sarah's neck.

"Hmmm." Sarah listened thoughtfully. "The Phlegmatics?"

"Wrong."

"Wait, wait, I know. It's that chap you like so well, Gordo Sax, right?"

"Nope." Pam tugged on Sarah's skirt, then clipped one enormous gold earring to her ear.

"Ow," Sarah said. The earring hung down to her shoulder.

"Try another song," Pam instructed. "I'll put on an easy one."

"There is nothing but earth and sky. Rabbits burrow and eagles fly. There is nothing but you and I. Life goes in circles."

"Oh, oh, I know this one," Sarah said, reaching up to feel her mountain of hair. "It's Birdbath."

"That's Bloodbath, Sarah," Pam said. "And you're wrong."

"Oh," Sarah hung her head. Her hair didn't move. "Oh, dear."

"Don't worry, Your Highness. You'll learn it," I said.

I could tell Pam was absolutely losing patience. She's the kind of person who likes everything to be done one, two, three.

I didn't want Sarah to get depressed. "I think you're doing great," I told her.

"You two have been so kind," Sarah said. "I hope I have the fortitude to continue."

"Why don't you try that opening Pam taught you," I suggested. "We can go back to the groups later. Right, Pam?" I gave her a hard look.

"Oh, yeah, sure, right," Pam agreed. She closed her eyes and shook her head at me, which was supposed to mean that this wasn't going very well. I ignored her.

"Sit over here," I said to Sarah. "And just relax."

"Very well." Sarah wriggled in her ultra-clingy skirt over to Pam's desk chair. After a number of attempts, she actually managed to sit down, hanging on to the hem so the whole skirt wouldn't ride up over her behind. Then she crossed her incredibly long legs at the ankles, tugged at her earring, and sighed. She looked absolutely miserable.

"Go on," Pam said.

"You can do it," I encouraged.

Sarah took a deep breath. Pam and I waited.

"Oh, come on, Sarah," Pam said.

"Okay, okay. Here I go." Sarah breathed again. I felt like I was watching someone get ready to jump out of an airplane.

"Cowabingo, ladies and gentlemen," Sarah began.

"Sarah, no D.J. would ever say 'ladies and gentlemen,' " Pam interrupted.

"Oh, all right," Sarah said. "Cowabingo, boys and girls."

"Sarah," Pam interrupted again. " 'Boys and girls' sounds completely dorfy. Say 'dudes and dudettes.' And it's cowa*bunga*, not cowa*bingo*. Geez."

"Sorry," Sarah mumbled.

"It's okay," I said. "Try again."

"Cowabunga, dudes and dudettes," Sarah said sadly. "This is — "

"Slammin' Sarah," Pam cut in.

"Slammin' Sarah with some . . ."

"Boffo hits," Pam coached. "For all you . . . for all you . . . come on, Sarah, you know it."

But Sarah just sat there.

"I'm utterly crestfallen," she said sadly. "I'm

afraid your diligence has been all for naught. This madcap scheme is doomed to fail. A disc jockey I shall never be."

Pam opened her mouth, but I jumped in before she could say anything.

"Come on, Sarah," I said. "You can't give up now. Not when you look so cool."

She did, too, in an odd kind of way. Most of the time, Sarah looks like she's wearing her brother's old clothes, which, of course, she usually is. But Pam had worked wonders. Now she looked like she hung out at concerts and rode motorcycles. Or would, if her skirt wasn't so tight.

"Surely, you jest," Sarah replied.

"I don't jest," I said. "Really, I'm not jesting." I hoped that sounded right. "Come on, Your Highness, be brave. Lord Ivo would never give up."

Sarah tugged at her earring.

"True," she said. "In *Quiet Comes the Dawn*, Lord Ivo says one must stand steadfast against even the most daunting foe." She stood up and wriggled over to the mirror to take a good look at herself.

"I can't believe what I look like," she said.

"You look like a WROK D.J.," Pam said.

I could have kissed her for that. It sure perked Sarah up.

"Well, perhaps I was just a little nonplussed," Sarah said, turning this way and that to see every angle of her new look. "Why don't I try it again?"

"Go for it, Slammin' Sarah," I said.

It was absolutely amazing. Once she relaxed and started to have fun, Sarah didn't sound half bad. She got the entire opening down so that it sounded pretty natural, and by the end of the afternoon, she could even recognize songs by Burn, Slugger, and The Accident. We had a little bit of trouble getting her out of her WROK outfit. Pam and I had to yank at the skirt with both hands, while Sarah lay on the floor gripping the legs of Pam's desk. But other than that, and the fact that the earring turned her earlobe green, the afternoon was a success. Sarah even borrowed one of Pam's Moonrush tapes to take home with her, and sang "*La, la, la, la, la, life goes in circles*" with me as we headed home.

It wasn't until I had said good-bye to Sarah and gotten to the linden tree that I remembered I was totally depressed. I must have looked pretty sad, because when I passed by her porch, Miss Frost told me to let a smile be my umbrella. The thing is, I felt like a dorf. I'd made such a big deal about the *Alice in Wonderland* auditions that every member of my family was bound to ask me how they went, and now I didn't know what to tell them. If I lied, and said they went well, then they'd expect me to get the part of Alice. If I told them the truth, then they'd say that I was worrying for nothing, and still expect me to get the part of Alice. That's the trouble with having your family believe in you. It's hard to convince them that you're really a loser.

Mom was on her hands and knees on the kitchen floor when I came in.

"Hi, Mom," I said glumly. "What can't you find?"

"What? Oh, hi, honey," Mom said, with her head in the pots and pans cabinet. "I'm looking for the blue salad bowl. Have you seen it?"

"No," I said. Then I sighed and sat down with my head in my hands. It was only a matter of time before Mom would pull her head out of the cabinet and notice I was upset. And even though I knew exactly what she would say, which was that I was worrying for nothing, and even though she would be wrong, since I was worrying for a very good reason, I needed to talk to her.

"Shoot," she said, crawling over to where we keep the canned food. "Where could it be?"

I sighed again, louder this time, and dropped my head on the table. Then I moaned a little. You have to be kind of melodramatic to get Mom's attention when she's on a hunt for a missing object. The moan did it.

"Beth? Did you say something, honey?" Mom asked.

I guess I really was feeling absolutely terrible, because I wanted to burst into tears that second.

"Oh, Mom," I started.

But just then Alison came bounding into the

room. Her little sister ESP must have been working overtime.

"Hey, big sister," Alison said. "Gee, you look lousy." She pulled up the chair right next to me and took a big, loud bite out of an apple. "So, I hear Kate did really, really great at auditions today."

"Who told you that?" I snapped.

"Kate," said Alison, chewing. "She called."

"Oh, my goodness, auditions. I forgot about them. I'm sorry, Beth. Let me sit down and hear what happened," Mom said. She smiled, waiting for me to say something.

"Oh, well, you know, auditions," I shrugged.

"Well, I'm very pleased for Kate," Mom said. "Things have been so tough for her these days, and she was so nervous. It must have been very helpful to have an old pro like you there." Then she patted me on the hand.

"Yeah," I said, pulling my hand away. "Sure. Well, look, I've got a lot of homework to do and . . ."

And I absolutely didn't want to have any more of this conversation. Darn Alison, anyway. I probably would have felt a little better if I'd been able to talk to Mom alone. But I could never say anything in front of my sister.

"Kate would make such an adorable Dormouse, wouldn't she, Beth?" Mom went on. "That would be the perfect part for her."

"I guess. I don't know, Mom. Anyway, I should go upstairs. I've got to get this stuff done and — "

"You know," Mom interrupted. "I should check the Small Town Players costume closet to see if there's anything for you all to use. I'll bet we have some rabbit ears, and I remember seeing a pinafore that you could wear for Alice. Oh, won't you look darling in that little blue dress."

"Just darling," teased Alison.

This was all too much.

"Look, Mom, nobody said I'm going to play Alice," I snapped. "I mean, it is possible that I won't get the part."

"Well, Beth, I'm sure that — " Mom started.

"Don't be so sure," I said. "Okay? Just don't be so sure. Gosh, you think you know everything."

The lump of meanness had reappeared out of nowhere. Mom looked at me kind of funny.

"All right, dear," she said evenly. "Why don't you go on upstairs, wash up, and start your homework? I'll call you when dinner's ready."

"Fine," I said, heading out the door. "Fine."

"Don't forget to call Kate back," Alison shouted after me.

Upstairs in my room, I shut the door and threw myself on the bed. Then I kicked off my shoes so that they flew across the room and nearly knocked over a lamp. I clenched my fists and stared at the ceiling, breathing really hard. I didn't want to wash up. I didn't want to do my homework. I didn't want to have dinner with my family and answer more of their stupid questions about these stupid auditions. And I absolutely didn't want to call Kate back. I turned off my light, put my head under the pillows and, finally, after holding it back all afternoon, I lay there and cried.

5

When I woke up the next morning, the lump in my stomach was still there, bigger than ever. It must have grown bigger and bigger overnight. By the time I got down to breakfast, it felt like it was the size of a football, and it's hard to eat with a football in your stomach.

My mom believes in a big breakfast. She says breakfast is the most important meal of the day, and that kids who eat a good breakfast do better in school, and that if you want to lose weight, the best way is breakfast like a king, lunch like a prince, and dinner like a pauper. I think the only reason she says all that is because she's too busy with the Small Town Players to make a big dinner every night. And also because after a long night at the hospital delivering a baby, Dad is absolutely starving. So we have huge breakfasts at our house every morning.

This morning we were having spaghetti pancakes, which my mom makes with leftover spaghetti and cheese. My dad won't eat bacon and eggs and other normal breakfasty food because of heart attacks, so my mom has to be creative. Usually I love spaghetti pancakes, but this morning I was too full of a miserable football-sized stomach lump to eat a thing. I just kept thinking about the cast list being posted today, and how I was definitely not going to be Alice.

"Aren't you going to eat those pancakes, honey?" my mom asked.

"Beth's on a diet," Alison said, stuffing her mouth full of spaghetti.

"I am not."

"Well, you should be," Alison mumbled with her mouth full.

I don't think I've mentioned that Alison is built just like my mom. She's real athletic and thin, and she does gymnastics after school. I'm built exactly like my dad, who was a football player in high school. My dad always says that with my broad shoulders, I could have been a linebacker. I don't think he knows how absolutely terrible that makes me feel.

"Well, I don't have to diet with you around, Alison, because just looking at you makes me sick to my stomach," I replied.

Score one for me. A big football-sized lump of meanness comes in handy for some things, I guess.

"Shut up," Alison whined.

"You shut up."

"You shut up."

"Both of you, stop it," my dad finally said. "Can't we ever have any peace and quiet around here?"

Just then he was beeped by the hospital, so he stomped away from the table, furious. Then Alison stuck out her tongue. Then my mom let out one of those "I don't know what to do with you" sighs. Then *I* stomped away angry. It was the absolutely perfect way to start the worst day of my life.

I decided not to take my usual route to school because I knew I would run into Kate or Pam, and I just did not feel like talking about *Alice in Wonderland* or WROK. So I walked the long way around, past Rumsey Road, where all the shops are. I was just walking along, looking into all the store windows, when I heard someone call out: "Elisabetta!"

Only one person in the world calls me "Elisabetta," and that's Vinnie from Deli Delicious. He was standing outside of the deli with his coat on and his key in his hand.

"Hi, Vinnie," I said.

"What are you doing here so early?" he asked, opening the door of his shop. "You want egg on a roll? It's the special this morning."

"No, thanks," I replied. "I'm not very hungry right now."

"Not hungry? My Elisabetta? What's the matter? Are you sick or something?" Vinnie sounded really worried.

"No," I said sort of sadly.

"Then you have troubles, maybe?"

"Yes," I replied. "I guess you could say that."

"Ahh, well, troubles I understand. I myself have troubles. You see this?" He pointed at his ankle, and I saw that it had a bandage wrapped around it.

"That's terrible, Vinnie," I said. "What happened?"

"I'm standing on a stool putting away some cookies. I'm thinking how my friend Elisabetta will be happy because I have the new cookies she likes with the chocolate centers, suddenly . . . BOOM . . . I'm on the floor, pain shooting through me like fire. The stool, it breaks right out from under me. They just don't make things the way they used to, Elisabetta."

I didn't say anything, but since Vinnie weighs about two hundred and fifty pounds, I wasn't all that surprised that the stool had broken. He claims that he likes his own potato salad too much, and I have to admit that Vinnie makes absolutely delicious potato salad. I've eaten quite a bit of it myself.

"Three hours I spend in the emergency room. One hundred dollars for X rays. It's a crime."

"Yes, it is." I couldn't believe it. Vinnie must

have the worst luck in the whole state of Connecticut.

"So, you want an egg sandwich?" he asked again.

"I can't, Vinnie. I'll be late for school," I said.

"Well, cheer up, Elisabetta. Remember, when you have your health, you have everything." Vinnie said, waving good-bye as he went into the deli.

I felt a little better after talking to Vinnie. I was thinking about being in the hospital, and how it would be an excellent learning experience for any actress, when I passed by the bank clock. It said 8:24.

School starts at 8:30 on the dot. Our teacher, Miss Moritz, is the strictest teacher in the whole school. She won't let you say a single thing in class once it starts, and she absolutely hates "tardiness." I started running as fast as I could, my backpack flying out behind me. I figured I could just make it before the bell, if I was lucky. I was running through the hall on the way to my classroom when I tripped. My history homework spilled out all over the floor. By the time I picked it up, the bell was ringing.

"Elizabeth Hanson, that's the third time this month you've been late," Miss Moritz said when I came in. She was looking at me coldly with her beady little eyes.

"Sorry, Miss Moritz," I said.

"Sorry just isn't good enough, Elizabeth. I consider three lates in a month to be unacceptable. I would like one hundred words by tomorrow on the importance of timeliness."

"Yes, Miss Moritz." I sat down in my seat next to Kate, completely depressed. Miss Moritz is just about the only teacher in America who will count you late if you come in five seconds after the bell. And she'll never let you explain anything. When other teachers get mad at me about something, I usually feel pretty sorry because I like most of my teachers. But when Miss Moritz gets mad about something, I just hate her even more. The lump in my stomach was like a basketball now, and hard as a rock.

"Tap tap tap . . . tap tap." It was Kate, tapping her pencil on the desk. Since we can't ever talk in class, the club has a pencil code. Kate was saying, "Miss Moritz is a big fat mean old hog."

That was one of the six things you could say in the pencil code. The others were:

> Hi
> Yes
> No
> Let's have lunch.
> Can I borrow a pencil?

I tapped "yes" with my pencil, and tried hard not to think about what was going to happen after homeroom. Mr. MacFadden had said he would put the cast list up at the main bulletin board by 9:00. In just a few short minutes, I will know my fate, I thought. It sounded like something Sarah would think, which made me feel just a little better, for some reason. If Sarah could bravely face the task of being D.J., then I could bravely face anything that came along. Couldn't I? After all, I asked myself, how bad could it be?

An absolutely stupid question, as it turned out. I don't think anything has ever been as bad as looking at that cast list with Kate and Abby. It seemed like a very, very long walk to the end of the hall. A bunch of kids were already standing there, looking at the list. Ellen Wu and Peggy Phillips suddenly screamed, then they burst into giggles and started jumping up and down holding hands. I guess they were pretty happy about their parts. Then Peggy saw us and came running down the hall, yelling, "Kate, Kate, you got the lead! You got Alice!"

For a minute, everything seemed to be moving in slow motion. Kate looked at me and turned bright pink. I couldn't hear her through the buzzing in my head, but I thought she was saying, "Beth, I'm sorry."

Then Peggy shook my arm and shouted, "And you got two parts, Beth. You're the only girl who got two parts, and Abby, you got a part, too. Isn't it awesome!"

Then Kate and Abby ran to see the list. I walked

over slowly, behind them. I felt about as awful as I've ever felt, but I didn't want anyone to know.

"Beth, look, isn't it great? We're all going to be in a scene together!" Abby shouted. "This is so exciting."

She gave me a hug, which I didn't return, and then hugged Kate, who was still very, very pink in the face.

Then Josh Baron came walking over, very cool. He just sort of glanced at the list as if he didn't even care if he got a part or not. Boys always pretend they don't care about anything, but I think they really do. He peered over Abby's shoulders, and when he saw the list, he yelled, "Yes!" really loud and pumped his arm the way tennis players do when they win a game. Abby saw him and smiled, and he smiled back and said, "So, I guess we're in a scene together."

"I guess," Abby replied.

"So." Josh leaned against the wall.

"So," Abby said.

"Well, see you in rehearsal."

"Yeah," said Abby.

Then he walked off. Then Abby and Kate screamed and started jumping up and down just like Ellen and Peggy. I stood there the whole time, in sort of a daze. It's not like I didn't know that Kate was going to get the part, *my* part, but I guess it hadn't really hit me until that moment. I couldn't even move because my stomach had turned into one giant monster-sized lump. Finally I took a deep breath and got up my courage and went to look at the list. I was going to be brave about it.

Alice in Wonderland Cast

Alice .... *Kate Tucker*

White Rabbit/Cheshire Cat ... *Charlie Goldstein*

March Hare/Queen of Hearts .... *Beth Hanson*

Tweedledum and Tweedledee .... *Ellen Wu and Peggy Phillips*

Mad Hatter .... *Josh Baron*

Dormouse .... *Abby Wagner*

There was more, but I couldn't bring myself to read any further. No wonder everyone was jumping up and down all over the place. Kate had the lead. Abby and Josh were in the Mad Tea Party scene together. Ellen and Peggy could stay joined at the hip. It was perfect for everyone except me. Sure, I was the only girl with two parts, but I got two parts I didn't want. One was the meanest, ugliest character in the whole play, and the other had giant bunny ears. Swell.

"Beth, I hope you're not upset," Kate whispered, looking pinker than ever.

"Upset?" I started to lie. "Why would I be — "

"Well, I guess we've both been earmarked for fame," someone interrupted.

I turned around, and behind me was Charlie Goldstein.

"What?" I asked.

"*Ear*marked for fame, ears, get it? I'm the White Rabbit, and you're the March Hare," he explained.

"Oh." Sometimes Charlie Goldstein's jokes go right over my head, which is kind of a joke in itself since he's about six inches taller than me.

"Congratulations," he said.

"Thanks," I said, not really listening.

After he left, Abby leaned over and whispered, "I think he likes you," in my ear.

That was all I needed. Charlie Goldstein is *not* the kind of boy you want liking you. He's really tall and he wears these very thick glasses and he's kind of weird. Maybe that's just because he's so smart, and takes eighth-grade math, and all the teachers are always *oohing* and *aahing* about his intellect, which, if you think about it, could turn anybody weird. Still, he isn't the kind of boy you want to have like you.

This was turning out to be an absolutely Vinnie sort of day.

Fortunately, the bell rang before I had to say anything to Abby and Kate. All through my morning classes I kept thinking about how unfair life is. And then came lunch.

The cafeteria seemed even more crowded than usual, and every single person in the entire school must have seen the cast list because as we walked through, everyone kept calling out, "Congratulations, Kate!" By the time we had gotten our lunch I was so sick of hearing about Kate getting the lead, I couldn't even eat my tuna fish sandwich. Not that the tuna fish sandwiches at the school cafeteria are edible, anyway.

"Boy, Kate, you haven't gotten this much attention since the time you came to school in those tight jeans and they split right down the back. Remember?" Pam said.

Pam hates it when anyone gets tons of attention instead of her. What she said was really mean. But I could have leapt over the table and kissed her.

"It's fun," Kate said. "I just hope I can learn all those lines."

I couldn't believe how stuckup she was being about having so many lines.

"Well, you'll just have to spend lunch hours in the library learning them. That's where Sarah is now. I sent her there to learn song titles," Pam replied.

"You sent Sarah to the library at lunch hour?" Abby said. "She'll starve to death. You know how much Sarah eats."

"It's okay," said Pam. "She packed about twenty sandwiches from home, and I'm sure I saw a chocolate donut in her pocket. Honestly, I've never seen anybody . . ." Pam started going on about the way Sarah eats, but I sort of tuned her out. I was glad Pam was there, though. I never thought I would be grateful to her for being so self-centered and bossy, but at least when she was around we wouldn't be talking about the play since she's not in it.

While Pam was talking, I pulled out my notebook and started to write. *Why Is Tardiness Bad?* I wrote. *By Beth Hanson.*

I was trying to think of an answer to that question, besides the fact that it could make you miss an airplane, when Kate leaned over to talk to me. "Beth, I'm scared," she whispered.

"Scared of what?" I said.

"Scared of being in the play. I didn't think I was going to get the lead. I thought *you* were going to get the lead. I don't know how to learn lines and get up in front of an audience and everything. Do you think maybe we could read through the script before rehearsal?" she asked.

Of all the nerve.

"Sorry," I said. "I can't. I'm busy. I have . . ." I looked down at my notebook. "I have this stupid assignment to write for Miss Moritz," I said.

"I can't believe she's making you write that," Abby said. "You were hardly late at all."

"Oh, well," I said, secretly glad for the first time that I had such a mean, rotten teacher.

73

"Yeow!" Abby suddenly yelled.

I looked up, and standing behind her was Josh Baron, who was pulling her hair.

"How ya doin', Blondies," he said to us all.

"Hi, Josh," Abby said.

"Well, see ya around, Blondies," he said, smiling his very cute smile.

"See ya," Abby said.

Josh is cute, I have to admit, although he doesn't have a lot to say for himself. But Abby has plenty to say about him. So for the rest of lunch, we all had to listen to her go on and on about how cute he is, and what he wore today, and what he wore yesterday, and didn't we think that sweater brought out the blue in his eyes, and should she wear her new black sweatshirt tomorrow . . . and blah blah blah for about twenty minutes. It wasn't my favorite topic of conversation, but it sure beat talking about the play.

I was starting to think that maybe I would make it through the day.

After lunch, I had glee club with Ms. Orpen, which is always fun, while the other girls took art and gym. Then came rehearsal. And how bad could it be? I asked myself.

I should really stop asking myself that question, because the answer is always *terrible*. First of all, I got to rehearsal late, because Ms. Orpen started telling one of her stories about escaping from the Soviet Union with nothing more than the clothes on her back. Usually I like Ms. Orpen's stories, but today I was just *not* in the mood. Abby and Kate had saved me a seat, but since I didn't want to make a big scene coming in, I sat way in the back of the room. Then, who should come in and sit down right next to me but Charlie Goldstein. He had this giant notebook with him, and while Mr. MacFadden was explaining about rehearsal schedules and learning lines and stuff, Charlie Goldstein was writing everything down in this teeny tiny printing that looked almost like typing. It was amazing how fast and neat he could be at the same time. My handwriting is so bad that sometimes I can't even read it myself.

I was so fascinated by Charlie Goldstein's notebook that I wasn't paying the least bit of attention to Mr. MacFadden and I missed my first cue. It was the Mad Tea Party scene with Kate, Abby, and Josh, and the whole time Josh kept winking at Abby, which I found absolutely annoying. Then Charlie Goldstein pulled out a candy bar and started to eat it right in front of me. That was when I remembered that I hadn't eaten one single solitary bite of food all day. And of course Charlie Goldstein didn't eat a candy bar like a regular person. He ate it in these tiny precise little bites, so it seemed to go on and on forever. I couldn't stop watching him. I missed two more cues that way.

Not that I cared, really. It's not like I wanted

to do the parts, anyway, but Mr. MacFadden started making jokes about my head being in the clouds, and everyone started laughing at me. It made me so mad, I didn't even bother trying. I just read all my lines exactly the same way. It was a lousy rehearsal. By the end of the afternoon, I hated *Alice in Wonderland*. It's a babyish story, anyway, even though Mr. MacFadden kept saying it was a great work of art. I mean, it has talking rabbits in it, for goodness sake.

After rehearsal was over, I walked out as quickly as possible without saying a word to anyone. I was halfway down the stairs when I heard Kate and Abby calling my name.

"Beth, wait up!" Abby yelled.

I waited. What could I do? I didn't want to be rude.

"Boy, that was fun, wasn't it?" Abby said, running to catch up to me. "I never went to a rehearsal before."

"Yeah," I replied.

"I noticed you were sitting next to Charlie Goldstein," she went on, teasing.

"Hi, Beth," Kate said as she caught up with us.

"Hi," I said.

"Did you notice? Beth has a new boyfriend," Abby said to her.

"Charlie Goldstein?" Kate asked.

"Yes. He was talking to her earlier today, too. I'm sure he likes you, Beth."

"Shut up, Abby," I said.

They both looked at me, kind of shocked. I don't tell people to shut up very often.

"Sorry, Beth, I was just kidding around," Abby apologized.

"Well, I don't like Charlie Goldstein, and you know it, so just leave me alone, okay?" I said.

"Okay."

"Beth, I was wondering if maybe I could come over to your house this afternoon so you could help me with my lines?" Kate asked. "I'm really nervous about learning so many — "

"Well, you should have thought of that before you tried out, Kate. Being in a play is a big responsibility," I said.

"I know it is, Beth. That's why I thought you could — "

"Well, I can't today."

"Oh. Okay," Kate said.

I knew she was hurt. I knew Abby was confused. I knew I was being really mean. But I just didn't care. And when they wanted to stop at Cone Heaven for a sundae, I told them I had to be home early. Even though I was hungry enough to eat a Blondie Special, which is a scoop of toffee crunch ice cream with caramel sauce on a blondie — you know, those things that are like brownies, only they're vanilla.

I just hoped my mom would have something decent for dinner.

6

This is what happened when I got home that afternoon.

1. Five ladies in leotards were dancing in my living room.
2. They were also singing.
3. I tripped over my sister's Barbie Doll Dream Vacation Houseboat on my way upstairs; and
4. got this huge ugly scratch on my right leg.
5. It really hurt.
6. My mom asked me to fold the laundry.
7. While folding it, I discovered my favorite white sweater had turned pink.
8. And shrank.
9. I stepped on a thumbtack. (See 5.)
10. There was nothing for dinner.

It wasn't until I thought they were going to find me dead on the floor from starvation that my mom ended the rehearsal and sent out for Chinese food. I was just about to dig into my absolutely favorite stir-fried noodles when the doorbell rang.

"I wonder who that could be?" Mom said, getting up to answer it.

I was too busy stuffing noodles into my mouth to pay much attention, until I heard my mother out in the hall. "Why, Kate, how nice. We were just eating dinner. Would you like to join us?"

"No, thank you, Mrs. Hanson. I just wanted to talk to Beth for a second. Is she home?"

"Certainly, Kate. I'll get her." Mom walked up to the kitchen doorway and yelled, "Beth! Company!"

Kate. Talk about the absolutely last person on earth I wanted to see.

"Hi, Beth," Kate said shyly as I went out into the hall.

"Hi, what's up?" I asked.

"I was just wondering if you could help me out, about the play and all," she said, "that is, if you don't have too much homework."

"Gosh, Kate. I'd love to, really. But, um, my mom asked me to, um, go grocery shopping with her," I lied.

"Tonight?" Kate asked.

"Yeah, you know, the supermarket's empty now and everything. Why don't you ask Abby to help?"

"I did. They're all out tonight. It's her mom's birthday."

Kate looked so sad and lost that I almost felt sorry for her. "Are you mad at me about something, Beth?"

"Mad. At you? Of course not, why would I be?" I said. Just because you stole the lead in the play right out from under my nose, and now you want me to help you? I thought.

"I don't know, you just seem sort of . . ." Kate shrugged her shoulders and started walking out the door. I almost stopped her. I almost said, "Come on in, we'll practice all our lines together." But I didn't.

"See you tomorrow," I said instead.

"Yeah, tomorrow," Kate said.

I shut the door behind me. I felt sort of funny. Not angry, the way I'd felt all day, but rotten and miserable anyway. I'd thought that being in a play with my best friends would be fun, but instead it was making me hate everyone.

I went back into the kitchen to finish my dinner. That's when I received the final blow of the day. My plate was completely empty.

"What happened to my noodles?" I said.

"I ate 'em," Alison said. "I thought you were finished anyway."

"WHAT?! You did WHAT?!" I shouted. I couldn't believe it. There was some kind of conspiracy to starve me to death.

"Don't shout at your sister, Beth. She didn't know you wanted them," Dad said.

"She did too know. She did it on purpose. She's just a rotten little brat, and you always stick up for her!" I was practically crying.

"Beth!" Mom sounded surprised. I was kind of surprised myself, since I usually hate fighting.

"Oh, just leave me alone. All of you!" I said, slamming the kitchen door as I ran upstairs and locked myself in my room. I just wanted to lie down in the dark forever.

Of course once I got there, my stomach started growling like crazy. But there was no way I was going back down there to say I was sorry to any of them. I would probably die of starvation. It would serve them all right. I bet Mr. MacFadden would feel really guilty at my funeral.

After a while, I sort of drifted off into a dream where I was wandering through a forest wearing a blue dress and a white pinafore, and Charlie Goldstein came hopping by in these huge bunny ears eating a bowl of chocolate-covered raisins, one raisin at a time. I was just about to reach in and grab a handful when this pounding at the door woke me up.

"What!" I yelled. This was getting ridiculous. I couldn't even *dream* about eating without someone interrupting me.

"Hi." It was Alison, of all people, sticking her head in the door.

"What do *you* want?" I asked. I was too tired to even kick her out.

"I just thought you might want some ice cream," she said, holding out a carton of toffee crunch and a carton of rocky road.

"Well, yeah, actually I would," I said. I was too hungry to worry about how mad I was at her.

"I brought spoons, too." Alison came in and sat down at my desk and handed me a spoon. "Which do you want?"

Toffee crunch is my favorite, but I knew it was Alison's, too. For some reason I said, "Rocky road."

She gave me the carton and we ate, not saying anything for a while. In my whole life nothing ever tasted so delicious as that carton of rocky road ice cream.

"How come you brought me ice cream?" I said.

"Dunno," Alison replied.

"Oh."

"Do you want to play Barbie dolls with me?" Alison asked, sort of shyly.

"Sure, why not?" I said.

So she went and got her Barbie dolls and we spent the rest of the evening playing "Barbie's wedding," and "Barbie's first day at school," and "Barbie gets a part in a Small Town Players production and really stinks," until we were both laughing and laughing, like we used to when we were little. After a while Mom called up from downstairs that it was Alison's bedtime, so she packed up her dolls and started to go.

"Hey, Alley Cat," I said. Sometimes I call her that.

"Yeah?" she said.

"Thanks for the ice cream," I said.

"You're welcome. Good night," she said and she walked out the door and into her room. Sisters. Just when you think you've got them figured out, they can sure surprise you.

That night I lay in bed thinking about everything that had happened to me in just two short days. I couldn't believe it was only the day before that I had been so excited about going to auditions. Now the thought of going to school made me absolutely nauseated. And being absolutely nauseous gave me a fantastic idea.

The next morning I woke up really early, going over my plan in my head. After a while I heard my mom knock at the door. She stuck her head halfway in.

"Beth, it's time to get up," she said.

"Ooooh," I said, giving it all I had. "I really don't feel well this morning, Mom."

"What's the matter?" Mom said, walking into the room and putting her hand on my forehead to check for fever.

"My stomach feels all gross," I said, moaning a little for effect.

"Well, maybe you shouldn't go to school today if you're coming down with something. You don't have any tests, do you?" Mom looked at me sort of suspiciously. She doesn't mind it too much if Alison or I miss a day of school occasionally because both of us get very good grades, so even if we're not really really sick, she'll let us stay home. But she'll never let us miss anything important like a test.

"No, I don't have anything like that," I said.

"Well, okay," she said, "if you're really not up to it."

"Thanks," I said weakly.

"Well, you get some rest, honey. I guess you won't be wanting anything for breakfast if your stomach aches."

"No, I guess not," I sighed. What a jerk I was. I should have said I had a sore throat or an earache. Now I wouldn't get anything but tea and saltines all day.

"Okay. I'll come check on you later," Mom said as she closed the door.

Hurray! I could spend the entire day watching soap operas and reruns of *Bewitched* and I wouldn't have to think about *Alice in Wonderland* for one single minute. I snuggled back down into my bed and for the first time since Monday's audition, I fell right to sleep without a single worry.

After a while my mom came knocking on the door.

"Hi," I said.

Mom was watching me with a sort of funny look in her eye. "Guess who I ran into at the drugstore this morning?" she said.

"Who?" I said.

"Nan Tucker," Mom replied.

Nan Tucker is Kate's mother.

"Oh," I said nervously.

"She said I must have been very pleased that you got two parts in the school play," Mom continued.

"Oh."

"She also said how proud she was of Kate getting the lead."

"Yeah, it's great, isn't it?" I lied, smiling falsely.

"Well, I don't know, honey. You really wanted that part, didn't you?" Mom said.

"Nahh, not really," I lied again.

"Okay," Mom said, but I could tell she didn't believe me. "You're not missing a rehearsal today, are you?" she went on.

"No, they're not rehearsing my scenes today," I said. That wasn't a lie, exactly. I did have one scene today, but I figured I could miss that, and Mr. MacFadden wasn't doing my other scenes until Friday afternoon. If I could stretch this stomach ache thing out until then, I'd have it made.

"Well, okay then. Do you want some tea?" Mom said.

"Sure," I said.

Mom gave me one more kind of funny look and went back downstairs. I think maybe she knew that it wasn't my stomach that was hurting.

For the next two days I worked incredibly hard at pretending to be sick. I pushed my tea and crackers away after a few bites, saying I didn't want any. I went into the bathroom and made gagging sounds when I was sure someone could hear, preferably Alison, so it would gross her out. I stayed in my room all through dinner, and, at night when the phone rang, I pretended to be asleep so that if it was one of the club, I wouldn't have to talk to them. Mom kept giving me these worried looks, and I don't think it was my stomach that worried her. I didn't care. I was hungry and I was bored and I was tired of pretending, but at least I didn't have to hear about how wonderfully rehearsals were going. Plus I lost about seven pounds. It's not a diet I would really recommend, though.

By Thursday night I knew I couldn't go without eating anymore, so I told my mom I was feeling much better and I ate my first real meal in three days. Then I lay awake all night, tossing and turning, until she got me up for school the next day.

When I got to homeroom, the club came running over to me.

"Beth, you lucky dorfball, you got two days off!" Pam said.

"Beth, hi! Are you feeling better?" Abby said.

"Hi, Beth," Kate said. I didn't even answer her, but I don't think anybody noticed.

"Josh asked me if I wanted to go over lines with him after school yesterday, and then he bought me a coke at Cone Heaven," Abby said.

"Wow, that's great, Abs," I said.

"You missed a really hard rehearsal," Abby went on. "None of us could remember any of our lines, and Mr. MacFadden made us promise to learn them by today." She looked at me very worried. "Do you know your lines for today's scene?" she asked. "Because that was one of the things I wanted to tell you on the phone."

"Yeah, I learned them while I was home," I said. I did, too. Learning lines is kind of easy for me, and I didn't have anything else to do.

"Pamela and Sarah have been working every night at Pam's house, getting Sarah ready to be a D.J.," Abby continued, pulling on Pam's braid. "We're all going to meet at my house tomorrow afternoon to listen to the show. Sarah's taping it in the morning. You can come, can't you?"

"Sure," I said. I couldn't let Sarah and Pam down. They were the only friends I had right then who I wasn't mad at.

"Oh, great! Sarah says — "

Just then Miss Moritz walked in, so I never got to find out what Sarah said. So far, I didn't feel too awful. Maybe I would get through this after all. I mean, what could happen in English class that would be so terrible?

Well, for one thing, there could be a pop quiz on poetry. I know Sarah loves poetry and everything, but I just don't get it. It always sounds pretty, but it never makes any sense to me at all. So what's the first thing we have to do when we walk into class but read this poem about some horse in the snow and answer questions. And Mr. MacFadden doesn't make you write the answers. He goes around the room and you have to answer them out loud. It's hard. So when he got to me, I said some really stupid thing and he gave me that "you could do better" look. But after Kate answered her question, he said, "Kate, that was quite profound." I guess she's his pet now.

The worst thing happened after class, though. I was practically out the door when Mr. Mac-Fadden called out to me. "Beth, could you come here for a second?"

"Yes, Mr. MacFadden?"

"I hope you're feeling better. We missed you in rehearsal."

"I'm okay," I said, trying not to be friendly.

"Well, while you were gone, I had Charlie Goldstein write down your blocking for you. Do you think you can arrange to get it from him before rehearsal?"

Blocking is where you walk and where you

stand onstage while you are saying your lines. I couldn't believe Mr. MacFadden had had Charlie Goldstein write it down for me.

"Yeah, I guess so," I said. I was absolutely in shock about this.

"Good. I hope you have your lines learned for today."

"Yes," I said.

"Okay. I look forward to seeing you," Mr. MacFadden gave me his best smile, the one that usually makes you want to smile back. But I didn't smile back; I just turned and left. When I walked out the door, Charlie Goldstein himself was standing in the hall waiting for me.

"Hail, fellow Rabbit," he called. It was so embarrassing.

"Hello," I said.

"Did Mr. MacFadden tell you? About the blocking?" he asked.

"Yes. Do you have it?" I said. All I needed was to have someone see me talking to Charlie Goldstein. He's so tall that every time he looks down at me, his glasses slide right off his nose and he has to push them back up. It's really irritating.

"Well, actually it's in my locker in my *Alice in Wonderland* folder, and I only have my English and math folders with me."

"You have a different folder for every subject?" I asked.

"Oh, yes, it's much easier to stay organized that way." He gave sort of a nervous laugh. "Don't you think?"

I didn't say anything.

"So," Charlie Goldstein said, "how about lunch?"

"Lunch?"

"Yes, I could give you the blocking then. I'll have just enough time to get to my folder before the bell if I take the back stairway instead of my usual route."

I wondered what his usual route was. I bet he had a map of every hallway at school, tucked away in a folder. Probably labeled "Map Folder."

"Fine," I said.

"Well, I'll see you then, at lunch. I sit at the table to the right of the fire door. I always like to be close to an exit. Just in case," Charlie Goldstein said. He gave me a little wave as I walked down the hallway. What a dorfball.

Then, of course, Abby and Pam had to tease me about it all through math class. They kept passing me notes with BH and CG in a little heart and stuff like that. I should have told my mother I had pneumonia and just stayed home for the rest of my life.

Sarah was the only one who was sympathetic.

"Beth, how are you feeling? You must have been most dreadfully ill," she called out when she saw me.

"Better, thanks."

"Pamela and I have been toiling away, attempting to better my efforts at radio announcing, but I fear she will be dreadfully disappointed. I'm in an absolute dither about the taping tomorrow. Did you hear about Abigail and Josh's rendezvous? I was so excited, I fear I almost fainted. Is that a Mystery Meat Loaf Sandwich?"

"Yes."

"Oh, fiddlesticks, I was so in the mood for Chili Surprise." Sarah's the only person I know who actually looks forward to cafeteria food. "Are you sitting down?" she asked, motioning to the usual NFBO table, where Kate and Abby were sitting and talking. They looked up and waved me over, but I shook my head.

"No, I have to eat lunch with Charlie Goldstein today. We have to go over what I missed at rehearsal," I said, hoping she wasn't going to tease me, too.

"Oh, dear. He's just a tad dorfballish, is he not? How dreary," she sighed.

"It's the worst. He has a separate folder for every subject and he maps out his routes through school," I said.

"Well, I hear he's terribly intelligent. People of great intellect are often rather odd," Sarah replied.

I wonder if Sarah is as smart as Charlie Goldstein. She's pretty odd, herself.

"Well, anyway, I told him I'd meet him at lunch."

"Oh, drat! I was so hoping to hear all about the play. We haven't had a moment's chat since you all became stars. I'm dreadfully disappointed."

For one brief moment I was grateful to Charlie Goldstein.

Sarah waved good-bye and sat down with the rest of the NFBO club. Abby waved at me and held up her notebook. She had drawn a big heart with an arrow through it. Of course Kate laughed. I wanted to kill them both.

Charlie Goldstein was sitting at his table, and all the plates on his tray were lined up in perfect rows. He had a big sheet of paper in his folder covered with tiny, perfect printing, which he gave to me to copy, so for most of lunch I didn't have to say anything to him; I just copied the blocking into my script.

Just as I was finishing my notes, Josh Baron came by the table. He hit Charlie Goldstein on the back and said, "Way to go, my man." Then he winked at me. I was so embarrassed, I couldn't speak. This day was turning out to be about as bad as I could imagine.

And that was before rehearsal started.

First of all, I was late again. I'd missed so much work in social studies that Mr. Raymond made me stay after class. By the time I got to rehearsal, I had missed my first cue, and Charlie Goldstein was once again filling in for me. To tell you the truth, he made a pretty good Queen of Hearts. He may be a dorfball, but he's not a bad actor.

Anyway, Mr. MacFadden was kind of annoyed that I was late, even though it was absolutely not my fault, and when I said it was absolutely not my fault, he said he didn't like my tone of voice.

Fine. So then we were doing a scene, and Kate just could not get it together. She kept missing her cues, and she couldn't remember any of her speeches all the way through. For some reason that made me really angry. If Mr. MacFadden had given me the part, I would have known it all. It would serve him right if the whole play was ruined. Finally, I just couldn't help myself. When Kate missed a line for the fourth time and screwed up her blocking, I said, "Gosh, Kate, get it together."

I guess it was kind of mean, but *really*, I just could not believe what a lousy job she was doing. Well, you would have thought I was the Wicked Witch of the West the way Mr. MacFadden looked at me.

"Beth, we don't need any more directors, thank you. Maybe you could spend a little more time on your own part and less on everyone else's. It's okay, Kate, just try again."

Well, excuse me for living. After that I was so mad, I didn't care what I was doing. I just sat on my throne and doodled on the margins of the

93

script. I mean it was *boring* sitting there listening to Kate do the same stupid lines over and over and over and never get them right. But then I heard Mr. MacFadden say, "Beth! If you're going to be in this play, I would appreciate a little attention to the scene."

So I missed a cue. It's been done before, and by people with much bigger parts than what I got.

"Sorry," I said, but I stuck my tongue out at him behind his back.

Finally it was all over. Mr. MacFadden was pretty mad at everyone, even though it was really Kate who'd screwed up the scenes.

"You kids just cannot keep goofing around. You have to learn your lines and start paying attention or this play is going to stink, and I will be furious," he said, pacing back and forth across the stage.

"Charlie, I told you a million times to practice your squeaky rabbit voice. One minute you've got it, the next you don't. Josh, you can no longer come to rehearsal without your script. The rest of you, please learn those lines. I can't say it enough."

He paused to get his breath, and I'm absolutely sure that he glared right at me. I noticed he didn't say a thing about Kate's performance, even though she was the worst of all.

"I need to have the following people come tomorrow so we can rehearse the scenes we didn't get to today," he went on. "Kate, Abby, Beth, and Josh. The rest of you I'll see on Monday. And for goodness sake, learn those lines."

"I can't come to rehearsal tomorrow, Mr. MacFadden. I have soccer practice," Josh said.

"Yeah, I'm busy, too," I said. Saturday rehearsal, what a ridiculous idea.

"You are?" Abby said.

"That's okay, Josh," Mr. MacFadden interrupted, sighing. "You don't have to miss soccer. We can work around you. Beth, why can't you come?"

"Well, I'm just too busy, that's all."

"Listen, Beth, you've been doing a very good job of playing a queen today. I just wish you would do it *on* stage instead of off," Mr. MacFadden said.

I was so furious, I didn't know what to say.

"Beth will be there, Mr. MacFadden," Abby said, grabbing my arm really hard and squeezing it. "She must have forgotten that her appointment was cancelled. Remember, Beth, you told me this morning." Abby was squeezing so hard, she practically cut off the circulation in my arm.

"Fine," Mr. MacFadden said. "I'll see you here at two o'clock."

Everyone started to get ready to leave, except Abby. "What is the matter with you?" she asked me.

"Nothing."

"Well, you're acting like a brat," she said. "Are you going to come to my house tomorrow to hear

95

Sarah's show? Or are you 'too busy'?"

I wanted to say that I wouldn't go to her house if she paid me a million dollars, but I didn't want Sarah to think I was mad at *her*.

"I'll be there," I said.

"Okay," Abby said. "Be there at twelve o'clock. Paul's making chicken 'n' sauce kabobs for lunch."

"Fine," I said.

Abby sort of sighed, the way my mother sometimes does when Alison and I fight. "Are you walking home with us?" she asked.

"I can't," I said. "I have stuff to do."

"You seem to have a lot of stuff to do lately," Abby said.

I watched her and Kate walk out the door together. The lump of meanness was back, and bigger than ever.

7

Since I absolutely was not in the mood to go home, I waited in the girls' room until everybody had left. Then I wandered over to the stone bench outside the auditorium to sit down and think. This entire stupid week kept playing over and over in my head, and I felt like I might explode. What really got me was that everyone was acting like the whole thing was *my* fault. Right. Like it was my fault Kate couldn't act her way out of a paper bag, and Abby found the love of her life, and all I got was a couple of dorfball parts that made me look like a complete jerk.

Well, this was the last play I was ever going to be in, I decided. The very last one. Ever. At least until I leave Connecticut and become a big star on Broadway. Then, everyone from South Meadow will come buy tickets and tell all their friends they know me, but when I see them standing outside my dressing room door, I'll just walk by as if I have no idea who they are.

And in the meantime, well, I'd just drop out of Drama Club altogether and join the Chess Team or the Audubon Society. Then when Mr. MacFadden suddenly realized what he'd lost, he'd have to come begging. And I'd say, "Sorry, Mr. MacFadden, but I'm off to look for the white-tailed wren. Why don't you ask Kate to help you out? You seemed so happy with her before."

It was becoming pretty clear to me that the meanness was spreading throughout my entire body. I had become one huge enormous lump, and I was starting to think that I'd stay that way forever. I felt as if I'd completely forgotten how to be nice. I began to wonder if I'd actually been taken over by aliens. I couldn't find my real self anywhere.

I sat and sat until it was nearly dark. Everyone in the whole school had left, even Mr. Rigby, the custodian, who locked up the building. My mom would be getting worried soon, and I knew that I should be heading home, but the meanness was so heavy that I could barely move. Using every ounce of energy, I hoisted my bookbag onto my shoulder and forced myself off the bench. I heard something drop and noticed that my *Alice in Wonderland* script had fallen onto the grass.

Stupid thing. I should just leave it there, I thought to myself, and instead of picking the script up, I kicked it. It didn't go too far, so I kicked it again.

"Stupid, stupid, stupid play," I mumbled to myself. "I hate it. I hate it. I hate it." Then I kicked the script once more.

Kicking the script felt better than anything I had done all day. Before long, I was kicking the thing harder and farther, and I wasn't mumbling. I was shouting.

"Stupid, stupid play," I yelled at the top of my lungs. "I HATE IT!"

I jumped on the book, which was looking pretty muddy and grass stained by now, then picked it up and hurled it toward a clump of trees as hard as I could, screaming so loudly that my throat actually hurt. "I HATE IT!"

"Ouch," came a voice. "Hey, what's going on here?"

From behind the tree clump came a tall, skinny figure, pushing his bicycle with one hand and rubbing his head with the other. This was unbelievable. It was Charlie Goldstein.

Aliens hadn't taken over my body. Vinnie had. *I* had become the unluckiest person in all of Connecticut.

"Beth?" Charlie Goldstein squinted at me over his glasses. "Is that you?"

"Uh, yeah," I mumbled. "Well, uh, gotta go." I hurried back toward the bench to get my bookbag.

"Wait. Hang on a second. I have something of yours."

Charlie Goldstein pushed his bicycle quickly through the grass behind me. His legs were so long, he caught up in about three steps. "Beth, here. Your, uh, script."

He held up my copy of *Alice in Wonderland*, or what was left of it, between two fingers. A couple of pages dangled from the binding. "Sure looks like you were *hopping* mad," he said. "Wanna talk about it? I'm all *ears*."

Great. Just what I needed. More of his idiotic rabbit jokes.

"No," I muttered, grabbing it from him. I was a zillion steps beyond embarrassed. I just wanted to disappear. "Look, I gotta go." I started walking away as fast as I could.

"Hey, wait up. I'll walk you."

"What? Oh, no. Please. You don't have to. I mean, really. Don't."

"Oh, come on. I'm going your way," Charlie Goldstein said, loping along beside me. "Look, no more rabbit jokes, okay? I'm sorry. That was stupid. I'll shut up." And he took my bookbag and put it in the wire basket on his handlebars.

So, there we were, me and Charlie Goldstein. Though if it hadn't been for the clicking of his bike chain, and the feeling that something was looming high above me, I wouldn't have ever known he was there. He didn't say another word. I wondered exactly how much of my little tantrum he had seen, but I was too ashamed to ask him. I wondered if his head hurt from where I'd hit him with the script, but I was too ashamed to ask him that, too. I wondered what he was doing riding his bike around at school after everyone had gone, but asking him that could lead us to the other questions, so I didn't say another word, either. I just trudged along, wishing that we'd both be struck by a meteor and wind up with amnesia so that this whole terrible, horrible, absolutely rotten day would just go away.

After about ten minutes of this no-talking business, I was actually sorry that Charlie Goldstein had decided to shut up. It's not easy to walk right next to someone you barely know and not say a word. It sort of makes you feel like humming. It's possible that at one point he might have asked me a question, but his mouth was so far above my head that it was hard to tell, and I was too uncomfortable to ask him to repeat himself. So if he did ask me something, I didn't answer him. Then, of course, he probably thought I was really rude, so maybe I shouldn't blame him for not saying anything else.

If I hadn't hit Charlie Goldstein on the head with my script, I would have asked him what he thought of the play and Mr. MacFadden, and then we could have talked about school in general. He's on the basketball team, I think. Or he ought to be. And I would have asked him how he learned to write so neatly, and if he had to practice a lot to do it. I mean, I don't think that I'd be like Abby is with Josh and just sort of stammer around. I think I actually could have had a conversation with him. Of course, I don't like Charlie Goldstein the way Abby likes Josh. And, unfortunately, he had seen me making a fool of myself abusing a book. So we just walked on, saying nothing.

It figures that the first time I ever walk home alone with a boy it would turn out this way. It wasn't the way I imagined it at all. It was supposed to be spring, and I was supposed to be wearing my blue cotton sweater with the lace collar because everybody always says that it brings out the blue in my eyes. The boy was supposed to be a handsome actor, with long, black hair and green eyes, sort of a cross between Denver James, my favorite soap opera star, and Mr. MacFadden. And just as we got to my corner, he was supposed to turn to me and say —

"Charles? Is that you, dear?"

That's not what he's supposed to say. That was Miss Frost calling to Charlie Goldstein from her porch. I was absolutely shocked. I didn't know he knew Miss Frost.

"Hi, Aunt Emily," Charlie Goldstein replied.

"Aunt Emily?" I said. I was so surprised, my mouth dropped open.

"Oh, look, you've brought the lovely Elizabeth with you," Miss Frost went on.

"We're just coming from rehearsal," Charlie

Goldstein said. "Beth and I are in *Alice in Wonderland* together."

I waited to see if he would make another rabbit joke, but he didn't.

"Well, how nice. Elizabeth and I are old friends, aren't we, dear? Won't you come up and join us?"

"Gee, I, uh, well, uh."

"Oh, come on, Beth," Charlie Goldstein insisted.

I was surprised he said that, considering I'd whacked him with my script and all, but he was already walking up the porch steps, so I followed along. I figured I'd say hello to Miss Frost, and then say I had to go home. I watched while Charlie Goldstein leaned over to kiss his aunt on her wrinkly cheek. He practically had to bend in half to reach down that low. Then he pulled out a little package from his backpack, perfectly wrapped in striped paper. He gave it to Miss Frost.

"Why, Charles, how sweet," she said, opening the package. She was one of those package openers who take forever. First she spent about a million years pulling off each piece of Scotch tape so that she didn't rip the wrapping paper. Then she folded the paper up very neatly and put it in her sweater pocket. Then she patted the pocket a few times to make sure it was safely inside. You could tell that she and Charlie Goldstein were related.

When she finally opened the gift, she exclaimed,

"Oh, Charles, how lovely!" and pulled out a silver picture frame. "What's the occasion?"

Charlie Goldstein smiled. "I just thought you'd like it," he said.

In a trillion years, I never would have thought that Charlie Goldstein was the kind of guy to bring pretty picture frames to his old relatives for no reason at all. But I had to admit, it was awfully nice.

"Well, you two," said Miss Frost as she re-wrapped the frame in tissue paper and gently placed it back in the box. "How about coming inside for a nice cup of chamomile tea?"

"Oh, well, I don't know," I said. "I mean, I sort of have to — "

But Charlie Goldstein interrupted me. "Sounds great, Aunt Emily," he said, bending in half again to help her out of her rocker. "You have any of those oatmeal cookies?"

"Of course," said Miss Frost. She slipped one of her long white arms through Charlie Goldstein's and the other through mine. "I even have some of the shortbread ones that Elizabeth likes so much. Heart-shaped." With that, she gave us a wink, and since she was already holding on to me, I had no choice but to walk with her into the house.

I hadn't been inside Miss Frost's house for a long time, but absolutely nothing had changed. It still looked as if she had taken everything in the entire world and put it in her living room. And it still smelled like cinnamon and roses. Charlie Goldstein and I helped Miss Frost to a big over-stuffed chair covered with hunting scenes, where she sat down comfortably and sighed. On a little table with painted legs was a flowered china tea-pot and a tray of cookies.

"Thank you, children," she said, settling herself. "Now, help yourself to some tea and cookies, and then let's have a nice visit. Elizabeth, dear, come sit beside me."

"Well, you know, my mom is expecting me," I tried again.

It wasn't that I didn't want to have tea with Miss Frost. I just couldn't figure out what was going on. It's not like Charlie Goldstein and I were friends or anything. I mean, I had always figured that he was basically a dorf. I looked over at him, kneeling on the floor beside the little painted ta-ble, laying cookies out on the plates in neat, iden-tical rows.

"I don't want her to worry or anything."

"Why don't you call and let her know that you're here?" Miss Frost said. "The telephone is in the kitchen."

Walking past the little table into the kitchen, I noticed that Charlie Goldstein had put an extra heart-shaped cookie on one of the plates. I won-dered if that one was for me.

Over the years I have learned that there are ways to get out of doing something you don't want to do, as long as you don't mind being a little sneaky about it. For instance, in this situation, I could have just hung around in the kitchen a few minutes so it'd look like I made the call, and then told Miss Frost and Charlie Goldstein that my mom had said I had to leave immediately. But if I did that, I'd have to go home right away, and then Mom would ask about my day and I'd have to tell everyone about the horrible rehearsal and Alison would say something annoying and I'd probably feel miserable all over again. And, frankly, I hadn't been feeling quite so miserable since I'd gotten to Miss Frost's.

I heard laughter from the living room, and then Miss Frost said, "Oh, Charles." I guess Charlie Goldstein had said something funny. He actually had a very nice laugh. The bubbly kind that came from his stomach. It didn't sound dorfy at all.

I took a deep breath and, instead of *pretending* to call my mom, I really did call her. Of course, it was possible that she actually *would* tell me to come right home, but I didn't think so. I knew that dinner wouldn't be ready for hours, if there was going to be dinner at all, and I knew Mom would think it was nice that I was hanging around with old Miss Frost. I told her I'd be home in about an hour, and that I didn't have too much homework, and that Miss Frost had made chamomile tea and cookies. I didn't tell her that Charlie Goldstein was there, too. It didn't exactly come up.

When I walked back into the living room, Miss Frost was perched at the edge of her chair, about to begin one of the wonderful stories she always tells about her life. She motioned for me to sit down. Charlie Goldstein was sitting on the couch, so I chose this pouffy little stool at the foot of her chair. The stool was sort of uncomfortable. It didn't have a back, so I had to sit absolutely straight, and it was very low to the ground, so my knees sort of hit my nose. Charlie Goldstein volunteered to switch seats with me, which I thought was truly gallant since *his* knees would come three feet past his ears if he sat on the thing, but I said thank you, no. It was the first thing I'd said directly to him since we'd left school, and for some reason my stomach did a little flip-flop when I said it. I hoped no one could tell.

Luckily, Miss Frost was already involved in her tale. "You know, Charles, it is just fitting that you are doing this play. Performing is in your blood. My father was an actor, and, oh, how he loved to be on stage. Mother positively hated it. Couldn't understand it at all. And, of course, she'd never let Papa give up his day job at the brewery. But in the evening, after supper, Papa would hitch up the horses and drive on down to the old Jubilee Theatre. You know where that fancy new whatever-you-call-it is on Rumsey Road? The delicatessen. Well, that used to be the Jubilee. And a more beautiful theater you have never seen. The lobby was all mirrors, and there were huge painted murals on the walls, and in the center was a chrystal chandelier brought all the way from Paris. Oh, it was a magical place."

I closed my eyes to picture Deli Delicious as the old Jubilee Theatre, with horse-drawn carriages outside and ladies walking in and out in long dresses.

"Well, more than anything, Papa wanted Mother to take my sister, Edna, and me (Edna was your grandmother, Charles, dear) to see him perform in one of his plays. But Mother would have none of it. Papa would beg and cajole. It meant the world to him. Finally, on his birthday, Mother bundled us up, and we all rode down to see Papa perform. She didn't tell him we were coming. It was to be a big surprise."

Miss Frost stopped for a minute to take a sip of tea. Charlie Goldstein leaned forward and offered me a plate of cookies. The plate with the extra heart-shaped one! He smiled at me, and I had to admit that he does have a nice smile. I also thought his fingers might have accidentally touched mine very, very slightly, but I wasn't sure.

Miss Frost was ready to continue. "My dears, I will never forget how excited I was that night. The theater was crowded with handsome men and beautiful women dressed up in their Sunday best. Mother led Edna and me down front to our seats.

They were covered in burgundy velvet. I'd never felt anything so soft. Then the lights went down. I held my breath, waiting for Papa to make his entrance.

"Well, I waited and I waited and I waited, but he never appeared. Edna was starting to squirm in her seat. I could tell Mother was becoming quite agitated. Finally, at the very end of the very last scene, a messenger ran onstage. He delivered a letter to the leading lady, bowed with a great flourish, and left. The messenger was my father."

Miss Frost paused and looked deeply at Charlie Goldstein and me. "It was a very long drive home that night, my dears," she went on. "Mother said nothing at all. Edna cried a bit. We none of us knew what we would say to Papa when he returned from the theater. When we heard him come in, I remember I ran to him and jumped into his arms and said, 'Papa, I love you anyway.' He looked confused until Mother told him what we had done. But rather than seem ashamed and embarrassed, he broke into an enormous smile. 'Well, and how was I?' he asked. We all stood silently. How could we answer that question? Finally, Edna said, 'How could we tell, Papa? It was such a small part.' Papa bent down and took her chin gently in his hand. 'Edna,' he said, 'in the theater, there are no small parts. There are only small actors.'"

Miss Frost put down her teacup, leaned back

109

against the chair, and closed her eyes.

"Great story, Aunt Emily," Charlie Goldstein said.

I knew I should have said something, too, but I couldn't. My heart was pounding. I could barely even move. Miss Frost's story had left me feeling absolutely sick. It was as if all my friends and Mr. MacFadden and Mom and Dad and Alison and everyone else in the entire world were standing there, pointing their fingers right at me, saying three words over and over again: *"Only small actors. Only small actors."*

I guess I must have turned kind of green, because Charlie Goldstein gave me a strange look, then quickly stood up and gave his aunt a kiss.

"Well, it's getting pretty late, Aunt Emily," he said. "I guess Beth and I are going to head on home now. Thanks for the cookies."

"My pleasure, dear," replied Miss Frost. "And, Elizabeth, I hope you'll come with Charles again."

I could tell that Charlie Goldstein was looking at me to see what I thought of that idea, so I tried to smile, but it wasn't easy. All I wanted to do was get out of there and have some time by myself to think. I was suddenly so overwhelmingly ashamed. I felt like my deepest, darkest secret had just been found out.

Somehow, I managed to politely say good-bye to Miss Frost and get out onto the street. Charlie Goldstein was right behind me, carrying his bike.

"Beth," he called after me. "Hey, Beth, are you all right?"

"Well, uh, sure. I mean, uh, no. I mean, well, I have sort of a stomachache," I stammered.

"Oh." Charlie Goldstein looked confused. "I hope I didn't say anything stupid or — "

"Oh, no, nothing like that," I said, backing away from him as quickly as possible. "No. I just need to go home now."

"Well, okay. So, I'll see you in school on Monday."

"Right." Just let me out of here, I thought. I felt like I was going to burst or puke or something.

"Well, bye," Charlie Goldstein said, getting on his bicycle and pedaling off. I could tell, even though I wasn't looking, that he kept turning to look over his shoulder to watch me walk away. I felt bad. Really, really, unbelievably bad. About Charlie Goldstein. About rehearsals. About kicking my script around in the dirt. About Abby, and Mr. MacFadden, and . . .

Suddenly, I started to run. I couldn't get home fast enough. I was panting by the time I saw the lights on my front porch. I bounded up the stairs, past Mom and Dad and Alison, past a turkey and tomato sandwich, coleslaw, and a pound of Vinnie's potato salad. I absolutely, *absolutely*, had to call Kate.

8

When I got upstairs, I went into my parents' room, shut the door, and picked up the phone. Then I put it down again. Then I picked it up again. Then I sat and stared at the receiver until that voice came on that says, "Please hang up, please hang up," over and over. So I hung up. So far, as apologetic phone calls go, this one wasn't too successful. But I just didn't know what to say to Kate. It's hard to explain to someone that your rotten behavior was not *your* fault, but the fault of a lump in your stomach that took over your brain. It sounded bad even to me, and I had lived it. I just could not believe how jealous and mean I had been to one of my best friends. The only good thing I could think of was that the lump of meanness had melted away, as if it had never been there at all.

The door opened and I saw my mom peeking into the room.

"What's the matter, honey?" she asked. "Is your stomach upset again?"

"No." I sighed.

"Is something else wrong?" she asked.

"Everything," I said, putting a pillow over my head. "I'm just an absolutely rotten human being."

"A what?"

"A rotten human being," I said again, this time without the pillow. "A jealous, mean, rotten, uncaring human being. With a bad attitude." There, that seemed to sum it all up.

"Oh, my," my mom said. "Do you want to tell me what's going on?"

Did I? I thought for a minute. If I told her, we'd have to talk about it forever. My mom just loved a deep, important conversation with one of us kids, and frankly, I wasn't in the mood just then.

"Not really," I said.

"Okay," Mom said. "When you're all done feeling rotten, there's a nice turkey sandwich downstairs for you."

She blew me a kiss and shut the door. My mom never gets insulted if you don't want to talk about something. It's a nice thing to have a mom who'll leave you alone if you want to be alone.

I picked up the phone again and took a deep breath. This was *Kate* I was calling after all. I usually called her about four hundred times a week. How bad could it be? I dialed. The line was busy. I waited a minute and dialed again. The line was busy again. I waited another minute. This time, it rang and rang and rang. I hate it when that happens. What do people do? Hang up the phone and leap out the nearest window? This was getting me nowhere. I hung up the phone again, and it instantly rang. I always think that's absolutely spooky.

"Hello?" I said.

"Beth? It's Pam."

"Hi, Pam, what's up?"

"Listen, could you come over here and help me out? Sarah's crying in my bathroom, and I can't get her to stop. You know I'm not very good at that kind of thing."

That was certainly true. Pam didn't go in much for crying.

"Of course, Pam, I'll be there in no time," I said.

I ran downstairs, past all the things I'd passed on my way upstairs fifteen minutes ago, grabbed my coat, and opened the door.

"Mom, I'm going to Pam's for a while," I called.

"Okay, dear. Just be home by eight-thirty," Mom answered. That's another nice thing about my mom. She doesn't make me stop and eat dinner, and she doesn't worry about whether I've done my homework. She trusts me.

I walked down the street to Pam's as fast as I could. Sarah, crying in the bathroom? That wasn't

like her. She was usually so brave about everything. She did stuff none of the rest of us would
have the nerve to do.

Once she walked right up to this extremely
handsome guy on the train and said hello. He was
a guard at the Metropolitan Museum who had once
given her and Abby directions, and she recognized
him and had a whole conversation with him. I saw
her do it. She even made us all go back to the
museum the next week and take a tour of the
Egyptian wing with him. He was very nice, for
someone so handsome. Abby and Sarah named the
hero of the novel they are writing after him: Alexander. Anyway, Sarah sent him a birthday card
with a poem she wrote herself, and he wrote her
back and said it was very nice, and that he had
read it to his girlfriend, and she liked it, too. He
enclosed a picture of himself with his girlfriend,
and invited Sarah to lunch with the two of them
sometime. Honest.

It was hard for me to believe that someone with
that much nerve would be crying in a bathroom
about anything. I just hoped Pam hadn't been
mean to her. When I got to the house, Pam was
waiting at the door.

"Help," Pam squeaked. "She says she's in utter
despair and cannot show her face."

"What happened?" I asked.

"This," Pam said, showing me a letter from
WROK.

It was addressed to Sarah, and it congratulated her on winning the contest.

"What's wrong with this?" I asked.

"Keep reading," Pam said.

So I read on. "*Congratulations.* . . . *Hope you're as excited as we are.* . . . *Please come alone, or if you're under eighteen, with just a parent or guardian. Good luck and* — '"

"That part," Pam said. "About just bringing a parent or guardian. I promised I would go with her and help her out, but they won't let me into the studio, and now she says that without my invaluable support, she can't possibly face this arduous task."

"Let's talk to her," I said.

We walked down the long hallway, up the back staircase, and into Pam's room. Her bathroom door was shut, and inside I could hear Sarah, still sniffling.

"Sarah?" I said, opening the door. "Can I come in?"

"Oh, Beth, I'm so ashamed of this childish outburst, but I just can't seem to sto-o-op," Sarah said, starting to sob again.

"That's okay, Sarah. I understand. You're just having a terrible case of stage fright, that's all. I've seen it before."

"Is that it?" Sarah sniffed, calming down a bit. "It's quite overwhelming. I rarely weep so copiously."

It amazed me how Sarah could come up with these words even when she was so upset.

"Of course, that's what it is," I said. "But there's nothing to worry about. You're going to be great."

"Oh, Beth. If only I could believe you," Sarah said.

"It's true, Sarah," said Pam. "You'll be awesome. After all, you had the greatest coach anywhere."

Sarah laughed, and then coughed, and then blew her nose. "But I just know I'll never remember all those songs and all those groups. Birdbath and the Night Owls and — "

"Bloodbath and the Nightmares," Pam corrected, sighing.

"You see, it's hopeless. And after all your labors." Sarah shook her head.

"Don't be ridiculous, Sarah," I said. "You're just upset, so you're not thinking straight. Everything will be fine as soon as you get to that studio and they say, 'Action,' or whatever they say."

"On the air," Pam said.

"On the air," I repeated. "You'll see. I always feel like this right until the curtain rises, but then I'm fine, and you'll be fine, too, won't she, Pam?"

I gave Pam a nudge with my elbow, and she rolled her eyes at me. I don't think she thought Sarah was going to be fine at all, but she said, "Sure, Sarah. Everything's going to be cool. Really."

"Well," Sarah said, "Lord Ivo always says we must look our troubles in the eye and smite them with our swords." She sighed deeply. "If only I had a sword."

"Well, how about a cookie instead?" I suggested. If there was one thing that was sure to cheer Sarah up, it was sweets.

"Smite them with a cookie?" Sarah asked. "Do you think it will work?"

"I'm sure it will," I said.

So we went downstairs to the kitchen, where there was always something delicious that Lucia had made, and found a whole cookie jar full of oatmeal raisin cookies. I only ate one, because I had lost so much weight on the stomach lump diet and I didn't want to ruin it. But Sarah and Pam ate about a hundred, and I could see Sarah felt much better afterwards.

"Come on, Sarah," Pam said. "Let's go over it all one more time. And I promise I'll come over early tomorrow and fix your hair for you. Okay?"

"Okay," Sarah said.

"And we'll all meet tomorrow at Abby's and listen to the show together, right?" I asked.

"Right," Sarah said, and she even gave a weak little smile.

I took her hand and looked deep into her eyes. "Be brave, Princess. Remember the fate of your people depends upon you."

"Thank you, kind maid," Sarah replied. "You have been of great comfort to me in my time of need."

I waved good-bye and left. I was glad to have helped Sarah, but it made me feel even worse about poor Kate. She probably had stage fright, too, and I certainly hadn't comforted her in her time of need. Maybe she would be home by now.

I didn't race through the house this time because I needed to eat that turkey sandwich, but as soon as I was done, I dialed Kate again. This time there was an answer. "Hello?" It was Mrs. Tucker.

"Hello, Mrs. Tucker, this is Beth calling. May I speak to Kate, please?"

"She's not here, Beth. She's with her father this weekend. Do you have the number there?"

"Yes, I do, Mrs. Tucker. Thanks."

"Good night, dear."

"Good night."

I should have thought of that. Of course she was with her father. She spent every other weekend at his house. It was hard for me to remember that, since it wasn't too long ago that her parents had split up. That made me even more depressed when I thought about it. And now I couldn't even call her because her father lived in a town in New York, and even though it was only about a ten-minute ride from where we lived, it was still long distance, and I wasn't allowed to make long distance calls. I would just have to wait until we got to Abby's tomorrow.

The next morning I got up early, and Mom helped me make a big batch of brownies. My mom and I make these absolutely delicious brownies that are Kate's favorite treat in the world next to a Blondie Special at Cone Heaven. I figured an apology might go over better if I was bearing gifts. Then, while I got dressed, I looked in the mirror and practiced what I was going to say. Whenever I'm in a play, I always practice my lines in the mirror so I can make sure I don't look like an idiot saying them. I tried about twenty different ways of saying "I'm sorry," but none of them sounded right at all. I'd just have to hope Kate could find it in her heart to forgive me.

When I got to Abby's, her stepfather, Paul, was outside, cooking up a batch of chicken shish kebabs on the grill. He was wearing one of those big red wool lumberjack shirts, a huge chef's hat, and an apron that said KISS THE COOK on it. Paul's a little bit goofy, but he's really a nice man. He was slathering the chicken with the barbeque sauce his company makes, and singing the jingle from one of his commercials.

"Hi, Paul," I called out.

We always call Paul "Paul," even though we never call anyone else's parents by their first names. I don't know why that is. Maybe because that's what Abby calls him. I think he likes it.

"Hi, Elizabiz," he said. Paul has a funny nickname for each of us. "What's the matter, can't you read?" He pointed to the KISS THE COOK apron. So I went up and kissed him on the cheek, and then he made me taste his newest sauce, Jamaican Spice Flavor, which was delicious, like all his other sauces.

"Lunch will be ready soon," he said. "Abs and Pam are in the kitchen."

The kitchen was filled with jars and jars of barbeque sauce, and there was a big pot of sauce bubbling on the stove. I must say, I sometimes think *my* family is kind of screwy, but Abby's house is pretty wild, too. I don't know if it's worse having tap dancers all over your living room, or barbeque sauce all over your kitchen. Abby's mom was making a huge bowl of popcorn, and Abby and Pam were dancing to WROK, which was blasting out of the radio. Kate wasn't there.

"Hello, Beth," Abby's mother called out over the loud music. "Have some popcorn."

"Thanks," I said, taking a handful and throwing my coat on the chair that seemed to be set aside for coat throwing. "These are for the party."

"Oh, Beth. How great. Your famous brownies. Thank you."

I looked over at Abby and Pam dancing. I wasn't sure what to say to them. Abby had been pretty mad at me yesterday, and with good reason. I had been so worried about Kate that I hadn't even thought about Abby. What if she was still angry? How much apologizing could a person do in one day?

"Beth, come and dance with us," Abby yelled. She didn't seem angry at all. She seemed absolutely normal.

So I danced over to them. Pam was teaching Abby some new move that had a lot of hip wiggling, and for a while we wiggled around until it got so silly, we all started laughing. It was so great to be having fun with my friends again instead of hanging out with a lump of meanness.

After we collapsed at the kitchen table and had some lemonade, I asked, very casually, where Kate was.

"She couldn't come today," Abby said. "She had to go somewhere with her dad this morning."

"Oh," I said. Great, now I wouldn't get to see her before the afternoon rehearsal.

"Anyway, I think she probably wanted to spend some time learning her lines. She's having a lot of trouble with them," Abby went on.

Didn't I know it. And had I helped her out when she'd asked me? Had I even offered a word of encouragement? I felt like the lowest worm in the whole world.

Just then there was a big commotion outside, and Paul came barreling into the kitchen, carrying

Sarah on his shoulders and singing, "Hail, hail the gang's all here," in his big booming voice. We all jumped up and started to sing along and dance around the kitchen with them. Sarah was holding on to Paul's head for dear life, because he's about a zillion feet tall, and he was bouncing her up and down like a little kid. Finally he put her down right on the table and we all applauded and shouted "Bravo!" Sarah was turning about a hundred shades of red.

"Oh, please," she said, "I fear after this magnificent celebration, you will all be sorely disappointed with my performance."

"Don't be silly," Paul boomed. "I'm sure you were wonderful. Now, we'd better eat these shishes before they get cold. Grab a plate everybody, and don't forget to take extra sauce!"

Abby went to get plates and forks for everyone, while Pam and I asked Sarah a million questions about the show.

"Did you remember everything?" Pam asked. "Your hair looks great, by the way. I told you a can of spray would hold it. Did you remember your lead-in?"

"How was it?" I asked. "Were you nervous?"

"What did Ready Freddy look like?" Abby asked as she came through the door with a plate full of chicken.

"Oh, dear," Sarah said. "Let me catch my breath." She sat down in a chair and fanned herself with a napkin. Then she got this look on her face, the one Abby calls her "storyteller look." She leaned forward, opened her eyes really wide, and started speaking in a dramatic voice, between bites of chicken shish kebab.

"At first," she said, "I thought it would be a dreadful ordeal. I was quaking in my shoes on the way up the steps of the studio. Though my mother's company was somewhat reassuring, I could not forget that my dear teacher, Pamela, would not be by my side. But I knew I had to be brave and uphold the honor of the Not For Blondes Only club. With shaking hands, I opened the door to the studio. There in front of me was Ready Freddy himself, and a kinder, more gentlemanly fellow you could not wish to meet. He shook my hand with a reassuring grip. He was not a handsome man. In fact, he bore a remarkable resemblance to my Uncle Morris, the used-car dealer. But I found that to be quite a comfort in that dark hour of fear.

"Finally we sat down to begin. The studio became very quiet, and a scarlet light began to flash ON THE AIR, ON THE AIR over and over. I was fairly gasping for breath when I heard Ready Freddy introduce me. Suddenly my fear fell away. With confidence I spoke my lines as Ready Freddy played the songs. I'm sure I made no mistakes. Proudly, I was ready to finish my 'set,' as they call it in radio parlance, when suddenly — "

Just at that minute, Paul called out, "It's on! It's on!" So we never got to find out what suddenly happened, or what "parlance" meant, for that matter.

We all gathered around the radio and listened in absolute silence. Sarah was right. She hadn't made a single mistake. She had gotten all the group names and the songs right, and she'd even managed to sound almost like a real D.J. I was so proud of her, I could have burst. Pam kept grabbing Sarah by the shoulders and shaking her with excitement. After Sarah introduced the last song, Pam leaned over and gave her a hug. "You were perfect," she said. "Perfect! I can't believe it."

"Oh, Pam," Sarah said. "Please continue to listen, for I fear you may be disappointed yet."

"Why?" Pam asked.

"Shhh. He's back on," Abby said.

"This is Ready Freddy on WROK, where you pick the hits," the voice from the radio said, *"and I'm here with our D.J. contest winner, Sarah Stern. Sarah, you've done a terrific job today. Did you practice at home?"*

"Pardon me?" Sarah said, sounding confused.

"Did you practice at home?" Freddy repeated.

"Why, indeed, I had to," Sarah answered. *"For I'm not really a popular music aficionado. My friend Pamela coached me."*

"Well, she did a terrific job. You say you don't like popular music? That's unusual for a

125

kid your age. What do you like to listen to?"

"Well, actually, I do enjoy the ballet quite a bit, and of course I'm terribly fond of waltzes. They're quite romantic. You see, romance is my life. I plan on being a famous writer someday, and I think that all writers should have a true understanding of romance. And of course there is nothing more romantic than a waltz. Imagine stepping into a ballroom, your heart aflutter as you make your curtsy to the handsome Duke who stands before you, his black eyes flashing with desire as he" — Sarah stopped talking suddenly — *"Oh, dear, I'm afraid I'm getting carried away. I'm so terribly sorry . . ."*

There was a long pause. I think Ready Freddy was a little confused himself. But then he cleared his throat and said, *"Don't sweat it, babe. Romance is your thing. That's cool. Listeners, this is WROK, where Sarah Stern has picked some hits for you. But no waltzes today, right, Sarah?"*

"Oh, no!" Sarah said. As Ready Freddy's theme song came on, in the background we could hear Sarah saying, *"I can't believe I said 'eyes flashing with desire' on the radio. I'm such a dorfball."*

A commercial came on, and Paul turned the radio down. Sarah was sitting with her head in her hands, moaning.

"I'm so dreadfully sorry, Pamela. I just never expected to have to answer those questions. I didn't even know what I was saying. Can you ever

126

forgive me?" she asked, peeking through her fingers.

"Forgive you?" Pam said. "There's nothing to forgive. You were perfect. You didn't make a single mistake. You just got a little carried away about romance, that's all. It could happen to anyone."

Sarah gave a sort of snort.

"Oh, all right, not anyone," Pam admitted. "But, hey, it could have been worse. At least you didn't mention Lord Ivo."

"Well, I suppose that's a comfort," Sarah said. "Do you really think I was all right?"

"I think you were awesome," Pam said.

"Well, then, I suppose I *was* somewhat awesome," Sarah said.

Pam gave her a big hug. Abby and I both hugged her, too, and then Abby's mother said, "Is everyone ready for dessert?" and brought out a plate full of my brownies.

"Many thanks, Beth. Thanks to you all for this sumptuous feast," Sarah said, her mouth full of chocolate frosting.

Watching Sarah, I remembered that those brownies were really for Kate. Now she wouldn't even know I made them for her. Maybe that was better. Maybe when you made a sincere apology, you didn't need a gift with it. I hoped so, because I only had one more hour until rehearsal, and I was quaking in *my* shoes.

9

I passed the next hour worrying about what would happen when I saw Kate. I knew it was up to me to apologize, and that made me nervous since one of the main reasons I hate to fight is that I hate to say I'm sorry. Not because I always think I'm right, the way Pamela does. It's more a fear kind of thing. I think I'm afraid that the other person will start yelling at me. Or that they'll pretend to accept my apology, but keep saying mean things about me behind my back. Or that they won't want to be my friend anymore. I've noticed that some people don't mind apologizing. They do stupid, thoughtless things all the time and figure that if they just say they're sorry, everything's okay. But for me it's a big deal. And I was feeling pretty nervous about it all the way to school.

Abby and Sarah walked with me. Bounced, actually. Sarah was so proud of herself, and even though she said she wanted to come to rehearsal to "soak in the theatrical atmosphere," I think she mainly wanted to hear what Kate thought of the show, and see if maybe Mr. MacFadden had heard her. I didn't blame her for being excited, and I tried very hard to bounce along with them. But I wasn't exactly up to it.

It's weird when six lousy words absolutely change your life. Important words. Not like, *You're in big trouble, young lady.* When Miss Frost said, *No small parts, only small actors*, it just stuck with me. I spent a long time trying to figure out what it meant, and I decided it means that if you work hard, you can make any part important, no matter how small it is. But if you don't try your best, it doesn't matter if it's the greatest part of all. Being a good actor has a lot more to do with the size of your heart than the size of your part. If I wasn't feeling so rotten, I would have laughed at that. It sounded like something Miss Frost would say.

Kate was already sitting onstage, going over her lines, when we opened the auditorium door. I could tell she was still having trouble, because every so often she'd shake her head or stomp her foot on the steps of the stage. Seeing her so frustrated made me feel even worse. I wished that I had helped her when she'd asked me to.

Okay, Beth, I told myself. Go over and say you're sorry.

My stomach started to flutter at the thought of it.

It's just Kate, for gosh sakes. She's your best friend. So, you've been a big jerk. It's not the end of the world. Just go over and say you're sorry. Just do it. *Do it.*

I took a deep breath, and was about to cross the room, when Kate looked up. "Sarah!" she screamed, leaping off the stage. "Oh, Sarah, you were fantastic!" She ran over and hugged Sarah so tightly, it knocked the wind out of her.

"Ooof," said Sarah.

"You sounded so professional!" Kate went on. "I couldn't believe it. I mean, geez, the way you were just talking away with Ready Freddy. It sounded like the two of you were old friends. Oh, Sarah, I was so, so, proud of you."

"She really was amazing," Abby agreed, and turned to me, waiting.

"Absolutely," I nodded, in kind of a daze. I'd been so busy gearing up for a confrontation with Kate, I wasn't really prepared for all this excitement.

"Grazie," beamed Sarah. "Grazie mille." I think that's Italian for "thanks a lot."

While Kate and Abby buzzed about Sarah, I tried to figure out what the heck was going on. I mean, Kate didn't seem angry at me. She hadn't actually said hello, but she was mostly dancing around with Sarah, so it was hard to tell. I don't

130

know. Maybe I'd been making too big a deal about this whole thing. Maybe there was nothing to apologize for. I had been kind of nasty, but Pamela's nasty sometimes. I tried to catch Kate's eye, but she was still focused on Sarah.

"And, are you ready for the biggest news in the whole entire world?" she gushed. "Mr. Mac-Fadden said he heard you."

"AAAHHHHHH!!!!!"

"Holy smokes!"

"Can you believe it?"

"I'm positively overcome."

"You're so lucky, Sarah," I said. I sounded sort of forced, but not because I wasn't happy for Sarah. I was just concentrating on getting Kate's attention. I knew I'd feel better if she smiled at me.

"Well, so, what did he say? What did he say?" Abby asked, practically bursting with excitement.

But just as Kate was about to answer, in he walked, wearing a black turtleneck and worn-out blue jeans and looking a zillion times handsomer than I'd ever seen him. Usually he wears a jacket and teacher-type pants, but since it was Saturday, I guess he figured he could dress like a regular person. I have to admit, I gasped. It felt good to be in love with him again. I hoped he would notice that my meanness had melted. He had been pretty angry at me at the end of the last rehearsal.

"Well, well, well. If it isn't Sarah Stern, the

new D.J. on WROK," joked Mr. MacFadden, walking right over to Sarah and shaking her hand. "That was some show today. Bravo. You did us all proud."

Sarah turned as red as a fire truck. "Thank you," she said.

"I'm a jazz fan, myself, but my friend Victoria was quite impressed with your song selections."

I heard a little scream come popping out of Abby, but she pretended she had a cough to cover it up.

"She's a real Phlegmatics freak. I'm surprising her with concert tickets for her birthday. Front row."

Cough, cough. Now Sarah had joined in.

"I think you two have met Victoria, haven't you?" he turned to Kate and me.

Cough, cough, cough, cough, cough.

"Goodness," said Mr. MacFadden. "I hope my whole cast's not getting sick right before the play."

We all pinched each other very, very hard.

"Anyway, good going, Sarah." Mr. MacFadden put his hand on her shoulder. "Now you can relax while the rest of us work. Five minutes, guys, then we're starting." Mr. MacFadden climbed onto the stage and started to set up a table and chairs for our rehearsal.

"AAAAAAAAAAHHHHHHHHHH!" we all screamed again, but this time in a whisper.

"Victoria's a Phleg-head?" Abby burst out. "She's so old!"

"Really," Kate agreed. "I wonder if she always listens to WROK, or if Mr. MacFadden told her you were going to be on."

"Oh, I'm sure they listened together," Abby said.

"Just imagine it," Sarah sighed. "A lover's tryst. Willie and Victoria locked in the throes of passion. When, suddenly, they stop short their embrace and switch on the radio, eagerly listening as yours truly strives, however briefly, for her moment of audio stardom. I'm positively quivering at the thought of it," Sarah shivered happily.

"Me, too." Kate and Abby nodded.

I wanted to say something to Kate about how absolutely hysterical it was that Mr. MacFadden asked us if we knew Victoria, but I didn't. She didn't say it to me, either.

"Okay, guys, grab your props from backstage," Mr. MacFadden called out. "Sarah, why don't you take a seat in the back and let me know if you can hear clearly. And, Kate, can I talk to you for just a minute?"

"Uh-oh." Kate made a face like she was in trouble. As she left, I tried to remember if she had ever once looked me straight in the eye.

Gathering the teacups and cookie trays that I used in the scene, I watched Kate and Mr. MacFadden. The two of them were huddled in a

133

corner, discussing something pretty intently. A week ago I would have been jealous that Mr. MacFadden was paying so much attention to Kate, and that she got to sit so close to him and talk in quiet tones. But now I just plopped myself down at the table next to Abby and hoped that whatever Kate and Mr. MacFadden were talking about, it would make Kate feel better about the play.

"So, how's Kate doing?" I asked casually.

"What do you mean?" Abby sounded sort of angry, which surprised me. Though if she was feeling protective of Kate, I couldn't blame her. She didn't know the lump was gone.

"I mean, well, I know she was having trouble with her lines and stuff."

"Yeah."

"And, well, I mean, I'm not so busy anymore, so if she needed me to, I could, I don't know, help her."

"Oh. Well. You should tell Kate," Abby said.

I looked over to where Kate and Mr. Mac-Fadden were sitting. Mr. MacFadden was giving her a reassuring pat on the shoulder, and Kate was nodding. She looked pretty nervous. Then Mr. MacFadden stood up and turned to Abby and me. I smiled at him, and he smiled back. I'm glad he wasn't the kind of teacher to hold a grudge.

"Okay, folks. Let's get on with it. The Tea Party scene, please. Abby, you sit downstage. Beth, you're in the center there. Josh will be upstage left, and Kate, your entrance will be over there. Everybody ready?"

"Good luck," mouthed Sarah from the back as Abby and I scurried to our places. Kate waited at the imaginary garden gate until Mr. Mac-Fadden said, "Curtain."

Now *Alice in Wonderland* is actually a pretty confusing play, and the Mad Hatter's Tea Party is one of the most confusing scenes in it. The characters are so weird, and since the whole point is that nothing really makes sense, well, nothing really does. In other plays that I've been in, if you can't remember when your next line comes, you can usually figure it out just by listening very carefully to the other actors. I mean, if your line is something like, "Why, Henry, I'd be honored to be your wife," it's pretty certain that you say it after Henry asks you to marry him. But in *Alice in Wonderland*, it could just as easily come after somebody says, "Please pass the mashed potatoes." So when Kate started having trouble, I could understand why.

Kate didn't, though. I could tell by the way she reacted when she made even the smallest mistake that she felt as if she were the worst actress in the whole entire world. And the more she felt that way, the more she messed up her lines, so it started to seem that Abby and I — and even Sarah, sitting out in the audience — knew Kate's part better than she did.

"Would you care for some tea?" asked Mr. MacFadden, pretending to be the Mad Hatter since Josh was at soccer practice.

"How can I have more?" said Kate, as Alice. "I haven't had any yet."

I looked at Mr. MacFadden. Kate had said the wrong line for the third time, and I didn't know what to do next. Her real line was, "Oh, yes, thank you. I adore tea." Then I was supposed to pretend to pour some in her cup. The line she actually said came much later, and after that one, I was supposed to take her cup and hit the Dormouse on the head with it. So rather than do the wrong thing myself, I looked at Mr. MacFadden. He nodded at me, like he knew what I was thinking, and stopped the scene.

"Kate," he said. "You're jumping ahead."

"Oh," mumbled Kate.

"Do you know what the next line is?" asked Mr. MacFadden. He asked it very gently. It was obvious that Kate was pretty sensitive about this line business. She thought for a minute.

"It's not 'Can I have some more?'" she asked.

Mr. MacFadden shook his head. "Concentrate. I know you know it."

Kate looked at her feet. I wasn't sure that she

was exactly concentrating. I think she was sulking, actually. Anyway, that's when I had a brilliant idea.

"Oh, yes, thank you. I adore tea," I whispered very, very quietly.

She didn't hear me.

"Oh, yes, thank you," I whispered a little louder, sticking out my foot to tap her under the table with my toe. She lifted her head.

"I adore tea," I prompted, covering my mouth with my hand.

Honestly, I thought I was being helpful. All I wanted to do was make it easier for Kate.

But rather than say the line and get on with rehearsal, Kate said, "Forget it. I can't do it. Just forget this whole thing," and pushed herself away from the table and crossed her arms.

"Kate," Mr. MacFadden began.

"Forget it, Mr. MacFadden," said Kate. "I can't learn my lines. I'm a terrible actress anyway. Let someone else do it, okay? Everybody else seems to know my part."

And then she looked at me. Well, I'd been right about one thing. She hadn't looked me straight in the eye until then. But I'd been wrong about another. There *was* something to apologize for. Maybe even more than I'd thought.

I felt my heart sink through the floor. I wanted to rush over to Kate and beg for forgiveness. Mr.

MacFadden cleared his throat. "Listen," he said, sounding tired. "Let's take a break. Five minutes."

"Fine," Kate said. And she stomped out the door.

Well, it looked like it was going to be a very long five minutes. Nobody knew what to do. Abby sort of stared at the floor and shuffled her feet. Mr. MacFadden sat down on a folding chair and started making notes on a big yellow legal pad. I contemplated moving to Siberia.

Sarah smiled at Abby and me from across the room and gave a thumbs-up sign, but I shook my head and held my thumb down. There was a really loud silence in the room.

"Well, now what?" Abby whispered.

"Beats me."

"I bet Mr. MacFadden's going to cancel the play." Abby sighed.

"You think so?" I hadn't thought of that.

"Not much point if we don't have an Alice." She looked at me hard. "Well, I guess that will make some of us happy."

"What do you mean?"

"Exactly what I said."

"You think I want him to cancel it?"

"And you're going to tell me you don't," Abby said angrily. "Come on, Beth, be honest. You've been a total pain about this play from the beginning. Ever since you didn't get to be Alice, you've done nothing but make everybody else miserable. Maybe you don't care about the play, but the rest of us do."

I opened my mouth, but nothing came out. Probably because I had nothing to say. Even though I'd told myself a zillion times what a jerk I'd been, it sounded much, much worse to hear Abby say it. I wanted to tell her that I *did* care about the play. I wanted to explain to her that Miss Frost's story had made me realize how horrible I'd been. I wanted to say that I thought Kate could be a wonderful, excellent Alice. But sometimes telling people just isn't enough. You have to show them.

I stood up suddenly. "You know, you're right," I said. "You're absolutely right." And without waiting for a response, I marched out to find Kate.

It didn't take very long. There was a light coming through the crack under the bathroom door and, since it was Saturday and school was closed except for those of us at rehearsal, I figured it was Kate who had turned it on.

I pushed the door open slowly and poked my nose around the way my mom does when I'm sulking in my room and she wants to check on me. "Kate? Katie? Are you in here?"

"Go away."

"Can I just talk to you for a second?"

"There's nothing to talk about," Kate said. Her nose sounded kind of stuffy. I wondered if she had been crying.

"Could you come out here, please?"

With a bang, Kate pushed the stall door open and, walking past me without a glance, she leaned over the sink to look at herself in the mirror. "What a loser," she said to her reflection.

"You're not," I started, but she wasn't listening. She was pulling at the big *Alice in Wonderland* bow in her hair.

"Might as well take this stupid thing off. I won't be needing it." She was about to toss it into the garbage, but stopped short. "Here, Beth. Why don't *you* wear it? You can be Alice now."

"What?"

"Yeah. At least you'll do it well."

"You can do it well, Katie. You just need to — "

"Don't tell me what I need, okay, Beth? Just because you suddenly decide to feel a little guilty. I know what you've been thinking all this time. But, hey, I understand. I mean, you're right. I don't deserve the part. I *am* a bad actress. So, here. Now you can have what you want." She slapped the bow into my palm and sat down on the bathroom floor with her face in her hands.

It's amazing that just when you think you feel lousier than you've ever felt before, something comes along to make you feel worse. I felt so bad,

I could barely even speak. "I'm sorry," I managed to whisper.

Kate didn't say anything.

"Katie. I'm sorry."

I walked over and sat down next to her. She inched away.

"Look," I said. "I know I've been a horrible disgusting jerk. I know it. I was just so jealous of you, I didn't know what to do. This whole thing is my fault. If I had just — "

Kate shook her head. "It's not your fault. I'm the one who's ruining the play. It would be better if I just dropped out."

"Don't, Katie. Please."

"No phony pep talks, okay?"

"I'm not being phony."

"Look, I might be a bad actress, but I'm not stupid."

"Kate," I said, trying to get her to look at me. "Kate, you're *not* a bad actress."

"Yeah, right."

"What you are is a bad line-learner."

Kate snorted. "Same difference."

"No, it's not. I'm telling you. I used to have the same problem."

"Oh, Beth, give me a break. You're perfect on stage."

"Excuse me, Kate, but are you forgetting my horrendous performance as Scrooge in last year's production of *A Christmas Carol?*"

"What about it?"

"Oh, nothing. I only completely forgot the entire Ghost of Christmas Future part. Geez, don't you remember? I started jumping up and down, saying, 'Bless me! Bless me! I'm alive! I'm alive!' and I hadn't even been dead yet."

"Oh, yeah," chuckled Kate.

"And what about when I was supposed to be Paul Revere?"

"What about it?"

"Does 'The Red Sox are coming! The Red Sox are coming!' ring a bell?"

"Oh, gosh, that's right!"

It was great to hear Kate laugh.

"I'm always worried that I'll mess something up," I said. "But I have a pretty good trick. It's not perfect, but . . ."

"What is it?" Kate asked.

"I put the words to music."

"What?"

"Well, you know how you can always remember the words to a song, right? Well, I just stick my lines in where the lyrics usually go. Like instead of, *All that matters is that you are mine*" — I sang a line from one of Kate's favorite Phlegmatics tunes — "Think, 'Oh, yes, thank you. I adore tea.' "

"This is really how you learn your lines?" Kate was amazed.

142

"Absolutely," I said.

"*'Oh, yes, thank you. I adore tea,'*" Kate sang. "Wow."

"See, there you go."

"Let's think of one for 'How is a raven like a writing desk.' I always mess that one up, too."

"Okay." I thought for a minute. "How about that one by Melba Toast — *Baby I love you like my worn out shoes.*"

"Perfect!" Kate exclaimed. "Gee, this is easy."

"Yeah," I said. "And if I hadn't been such a brat, you could have done it a long time ago. Do you think you can forgive me?"

"We-ell." Kate hesitated. Then she gave me a hug. "Of course, I can."

For the next few minutes we sat there on the bathroom floor, trying to find songs to fit all of Kate's hard-to-learn lines. I felt happier than I had felt in weeks. We were really rockin' to "How Doth the Little Crocodile" when there was a knock at the door, and Sarah peered in.

"A thousand pardons if I'm interrupting an important rendezvous," she said apologetically. "But Mr. MacFadden requests your presence in the auditorium."

"Okay, Sarah," I said. "We're coming."

"And may I advise you that we have a visitor of great merit in the audience this afternoon." She glanced behind her to make sure no one was looking, then stuck her head in even farther and whispered loudly, "Victoria's here!"

"You're kidding!" Kate and I shouted at once.

"Shhhh," Sarah pressed her finger to her lips and glanced around again. Satisfied, she smiled broadly. "It's too, too thrilling, if you ask me. I'm just hoping to witness a lingering embrace before they leave."

"Just give us a second. We'll be right there," I said and then turning to Kate, I asked, "Ready?"

"Oh, yes, thank you. I adore tea," Kate replied with a smile.

"Let's go." I leapt up, but just as I was about to open the bathroom door, I stopped and turned around. "Wait a second." I pulled the white bow out of my pocket. "You know, I finally figured out why Mr. MacFadden cast you as Alice," I said, tying it in Kate's hair. "It's because you're the best."

The rest of rehearsal went absolutely smoothly, especially considering Victoria was there. It was very hard to concentrate when you kept wondering if they would start going at it, but somehow all of us managed to say our parts right. All of us, that is, except Mr. MacFadden, who kept messing up Josh's lines, even with the script right in front of him. At one point, when he was supposed to say, "The Dormouse is afraid," he actually said, "The Dormouse is in love." I thought Abby, Kate, and I were going to throw up, we were trying so hard not to laugh. Sarah had to get up and run out of the room.

Kate got better and better as the rehearsal went on, and after a while she could even stop humming under her breath and just relax. She looked so perfect in her little white pinafore with that white bow in her hair that I actually started to believe she was Alice, and I think she started to believe it herself.

After we'd done the scene for about the millionth time, Mr. MacFadden stood up and applauded. "There we go. That's the way to do it. Great work, girls. Excellent, Kate. Now you've really got it."

We all felt good. Especially since he'd said it in front of Victoria.

After rehearsal was over, he introduced us all to her again. Victoria told Sarah that she should consider a career in radio, and told Kate that she was positively born to play Alice. I could tell that Mr. MacFadden wanted to get going already, but we all dawdled around, hoping that if we waited long enough, he and Victoria would kiss. When he finally did get us out the door, Sarah pretended that she'd dropped her keys so we could stand by the building and watch them walk away together. It only took about three seconds before they'd wrapped their arms around each other and started snuggling. They must really be in love.

Sarah wanted to follow them, but Kate and

Abby had to get home, so we all headed down the hill toward the front gate. The soccer team had just gotten back from their game, and I could see Josh Baron and a bunch of his friends hanging around and laughing. I was just about to give Abby a nudge when I heard the familiar sound of a bicycle bell and felt a tap on my shoulder. It was Charlie Goldstein.

"I had this hare-brained idea that I'd come by rehearsal." He laughed. "Stupid rabbit joke, I know. Sometimes I just can't help myself."

I didn't even have to look at Abby, Kate, and Sarah. I knew they were pinching each other and giggling.

"Anyway," Charlie Goldstein went on, "I hope you don't mind."

He was as tall and gawky as ever, and his glasses kept sliding down his nose, but for some reason, I really didn't mind. I actually handed him my bookbag, and he put it in his bicycle basket, which made Abby, Kate, and Sarah practically scream, and then Josh ran over and started walking with us, and for the first time in a long while, I was absolutely happy.

10

"**B**eth, you've got to come over. It's happening again!"

It was Pamela on the telephone, and she sounded very upset.

"What's happening again?" I asked.

"Bathroom freak-out," Pam said. "Crying, stage fright, terror, the whole works. You've got to help."

"I'll be right there," I said.

It was Saturday afternoon, three weeks later, only four hours till opening night of *Alice in Wonderland*. I thought Kate was doing really great. We'd been working together on her lines until she knew them so well, she could say them in her sleep, and she was doing a good acting job, too. I thought she was feeling really sure of herself. I just couldn't believe she was crying in Pam's bathroom. Unless she was upset about dress rehearsal.

When you've been in a lot of plays, like I have,

you learn about dress rehearsal. It's called that because it's the one right before opening night, and everyone dresses in their costumes for the first time. It's supposed to be just like a real performance of the play, and you're not supposed to stop even if you forget a line or something, just as if there were an audience. The thing is, it absolutely never works out like that. Every play I've ever done, the dress rehearsal has been a total disaster, starting in second grade when Brittany Carlucci wet her pants right in the middle of the stage.

We had dress rehearsal for *Alice in Wonderland* this morning at ten o'clock, and even though I knew dress rehearsals never go well, I was sure that this time everything would be great. When I got there, the auditorium was what Miss Frost would call "a hive of activity." Josh was on the stage pinning the scenery to the curtains. He and Abby had done a great job painting it. Abby showed me this secret place where he had drawn her initials and his in a heart. It was so romantic. Sarah was sitting backstage with headphones, trying to learn the lighting cues. She had volunteered to do the lighting after our fateful Saturday rehearsal, even though she is "dismally ignorant of modern technology." She and Mr. MacFadden worked together for three whole hours, all alone, on Thursday afternoon. The rest of us were so jealous, we couldn't stand it. The next play we do, I'm going to think seriously about doing the lighting. Even Pam had decided to help out, and she was at the dress rehearsal with this huge makeup kit that Mr. MacFadden had given her, putting mouse whiskers on Abby.

Mr. MacFadden was running through the Tweedledum and Tweedledee scene with Kate, Ellen Wu, and Peggy Phillips. The way he directed the scene, it felt like the Tweedles were *supposed* to giggle every five seconds, as if they were just two giggly fat guys in funny hats. It was perfect for Ellen and Peggy. They were *so* funny, everyone in the audience was going to be giggling up a storm with them. Mr. MacFadden is a great director. I was sure this play was going to be a big hit.

As I walked up to the stage, I waved hello to everyone.

"Beth," Mr. MacFadden said, "have you seen Charlie Goldstein?"

"No," I said, turning a little red. Charlie Goldstein had walked me home a few times, but I didn't want anyone to make anything of it.

"He was supposed to be here early to help Josh with the scenery. It's not like him to be late." Mr. MacFadden said.

That was true. Charlie Goldstein was always on time.

"Oh, well, I'm sure he'll be here soon," he went on. "We'll just have to start without him. Get your costumes, everyone. I want you dressed and in makeup in twenty minutes. And then I want to see you all onstage before we start, okay?"

We ran around like maniacs, trying to get into our costumes in twenty minutes, but it was impossible. First the zipper broke on Tweedledum's outfit. Nobody had any safety pins, so I had to go to the Woolworth store down the street dressed in a bunny costume, to buy a package of them. I was absolutely embarrassed, but I was still trying to make up for my obnoxious behavior the first week, so I didn't say anything.

Then Josh tripped over his pants leg and fell right on top of Pam's makeup case and got "Luscious Tangerine" lipstick all over his white shirt. I think maybe he's spending too much time with Abby, because he's getting almost as clumsy as she is. Fortunately for all of us, Mr. MacFadden was wearing a white shirt, so he took it off and gave it to Josh. Right in front of everybody. He was wearing just a T-shirt underneath, and he had these really great-looking arms. Peggy Phillips giggled so hard at this that she got a terrible case of the hiccups and for the rest of the rehearsal, she kept hiccuping really loudly through every scene.

Finally, after about an hour we were all ready to go. Except for Charlie Goldstein, who still wasn't there. Mr. MacFadden called his house, but there was no answer, so we had no choice but to go on without him. I could tell that Mr. MacFadden was getting pretty mad, but I was actually a little worried. If there is one person in the whole world who you can absolutely depend on, it's Charlie Goldstein. I couldn't think of a single reason why he would be so late. Mr. MacFadden asked me to fill in for him.

We had just started the play when all of a sudden, the stage lights went out. It was pitch black in the auditorium, and all you could hear was Sarah. "Oh, noooooo!" she wailed. "What have I done?"

Mr. MacFadden managed to find the switch for the house lights, but not before he bumped himself really hard against something in the dark. I heard him mutter something under his breath. I'm not sure what he said, but I can guess. I don't think he was too happy with the way the dress rehearsal was going.

"Oh, Mr. MacFadden," Sarah said, running up to him, "I promise I only did what you said. I lowered light three and I raised light four. I swear on everything I hold dear that I did nothing else, and you know I would never deliberately sabotage your lovely lights, or in any way try to destroy the confidence you have so graciously placed in my abilities or — "

"Sarah, Sarah," Mr. MacFadden interrupted, laughing. Sarah just cracks him up for some reason. "It's okay. You didn't do anything wrong. I think a fuse must have blown. Does anyone here know where the fuse box might be?"

There was dead silence. Nobody had a clue about that, and without lights, how could the show go on? This was really turning into a disaster.

Suddenly a voice called out from the back of the auditorium. "Perhaps I can be of assistance?"

It was Charlie Goldstein. He was standing there with a smile on his face and a huge cast on his arm going all the way up to his shoulder. It was wrapped in a big sling, and he had a white bandage on his head. He looked as if he had been in a terrible accident.

As it turns out, he had spent the whole morning at the hospital after falling off his bike on the way to rehearsal. He had a broken wrist, and three stitches in his forehead. Mr. MacFadden wanted to send him home right away, but he insisted on staying through rehearsal, even though he must have felt just awful. When I was nine, I broke my ankle falling out of a treehouse, and it hurt like you absolutely can't believe. It made me feel as if Charlie Goldstein must be the bravest person I ever met, next to Sarah.

He's also the smartest, and since he's one of those people who knows everything, he knew where the fuse box was. So Mr. MacFadden sent Josh and Abby out to get a new fuse at the hardware store, while everybody else tried to figure out how to get Charlie Goldstein's cast into a bunny costume. It wasn't easy, and it involved a lot of cutting, but Pamela finally figured it out so it looked kind of stylish. She used a red scarf as a sling, and found a hat to go over his cut, and he looked okay.

Once the lights were fixed, there was hardly any time to actually rehearse, so we rushed through all the scenes just to make sure everyone knew their lines. It wasn't very successful, but afterward Mr. MacFadden said we had all done very well under "adverse conditions," which Sarah said meant all the bad things that had happened that day. He also said he was proud of each and every one of us, and that he was sure the show would be great. I love Mr. MacFadden.

As we were leaving, Charlie Goldstein asked if he could walk me home. Right up to that minute I had still been kind of embarrassed about him liking me. I mean, even though he didn't bug me anymore, and when he walked home with me I'd kind of started to enjoy it, I still felt a little bit funny about him being such a dorfball and everything. But today, when he asked me, I just felt proud. Charlie Goldstein might be a little weird, and he might be a little tall and skinny, but he was smart and he was brave and he was the hero of the day. I felt that I was a really lucky girl to have him like me.

So after a dress rehearsal like that, I could understand why Kate might have been a little nervous about the play. But I was still surprised that she was crying in Pam's bathroom from stage fright. She'd seemed so confident and happy this morning. I ran over to Pam's house as quickly as I could and rang her doorbell. She opened it in a split second. She must have been waiting for me.

"Beth, hurry up. I can't stand one more minute of this," Pam said, pulling me by the arm up the stairs to her room.

"What happened?" I asked.

"One minute she was fine, and the next she was crying in the bathroom. What is it with my bathroom, anyway? Is there something about the wallpaper?"

When we got to Pam's room, I went over to the bathroom door. I could hear sniffling and nose blowing, but no actual crying. Maybe Kate was feeling better.

"Can I come in?" I said, poking my head in the door.

It wasn't Kate in the bathroom at all! It was Abby!

"Hi, Beth," she snuffled. "Pretty stupid, huh?"

"Of course not," I said. "Not at all."

It wasn't the most helpful thing to say, but I was kind of surprised. Abby is usually so calm and collected about everything. She isn't the crying-in-the-bathroom type at all.

"I don't know what happened," Abby went on. "I was just thinking about the play, and being on stage, and all those people watching me. First I felt like throwing up, then I felt like crying."

"Well, gosh, I'm glad you didn't puke, at least," Pam said. "Do you think from now on we could have this sort of thing at someone else's house?"

"Sorry, Pam," Abby sniffed. "I feel a little better now, anyway."

"That's okay," Pam said. "I'm starting to get used to it."

"Don't worry, Abby," I said. "Lots of people get stage fright. You should have seen Sarah the night before her radio show."

"Do you think anyone else is nervous?" Abby said.

"Sure," I said. "I bet even Mr. MacFadden is nervous."

"Yeah, but Victoria's probably comforting him," Abby said, giggling.

"I know something you don't know," Pam sang out.

"What?" Abby and I said together.

"I was in Barton's department store yesterday, trying on dresses. I saw the cutest red dress with a bow on the back and a black stripe right down the — "

"Get to the point, Pam," Abby said. If you don't stop Pam when she's talking about clothes, she'll go on forever.

"Well, guess who I saw working there? In the sweater department."

"Who?" we asked.

"Victoria," Pam said triumphantly.

Victoria worked in the sweater department at Barton's department store? How disappointing.

"You're kidding!" Abby said. "I have to call Sarah and tell her. She was sure Victoria was a starving artist."

"She dresses too well to be a starving artist," Pam said. "She probably gets a discount on all the clothes in the store."

After we had discussed Victoria's career for a while, Abby felt much better. She decided to go home and take a bubble bath, which Sarah had once told her was the solution to all problems. I walked her to the end of my block, and then I went home. It was only three hours until show time, and we had to be at school an hour and a half early. I was starting to feel a little bit like puking myself.

By six-thirty we were all sitting backstage, in makeup and costumes, trying to be as quiet as possible. The doors were opening in five minutes, and it was "very unprofessional," according to Mr. MacFadden, to have any backstage noise, even while the audience was coming in and couldn't hear you anyway. Last year, when Mrs. Adrian directed the Thanksgiving play, everyone was running around backstage like crazy beforehand, looking through the curtains to see if their parents had come yet, and even waving to them if they had. Nobody knew their lines very well, either, so Mrs. Adrian kept a script backstage and prompted us if we forgot them. Mr. MacFadden wasn't doing anything like that, and he would have been furious if we'd waved at our parents. He expected us to behave like real professional actors. And the thing is, we all wanted him to be proud of us, so we were really trying.

It was hard, though. The only person who could see out into the audience was Sarah in the lighting booth, so she would call back to us if someone interesting came in.

"Beth," she said, "I see your mother and Alison, but I don't see your father."

It figured. My dad probably had to go to the hospital. He's missed almost every show I've ever been in.

"Kate, your mother is here!" Sarah called.

I looked over at Kate. She was sitting in a corner, mumbling something under her breath. I leaned over to hear.

"What is the use of a book without pictures or conversation . . . what is the use of a book without pictures or conversation . . . what is the use of a book . . ." she was saying over and over again. It was her first line in the play.

"Don't worry," I whispered, squeezing her hand, "you're going to be great."

"Victoria has arrived," Sarah called to us. "Mr. MacFadden is greeting her now."

We all waited breathlessly. Peggy and Ellen started to giggle again.

"Kiss on the cheek," Sarah called. "How dreadfully disappointing. Pam must be correct about her employment, however, for she is wearing a terribly pretty sweater. Oh, he's coming backstage now. Peggy, I'd advise you to compose yourself. You don't want to start hicupping again."

Peggy started to take deep breaths. Mr. MacFadden walked through the backstage entrance and waved hello.

"Hi," we all whispered.

"Everyone, I want you to know that I'm very, very proud of you all, and I know you're going to do a great job. Break a leg, everyone. Except Charlie Goldstein — you've broken enough bones today, okay?"

We all laughed. "Break a leg" is what you say in the theater when you mean "good luck," because to say "good luck" is supposed to be bad luck. I don't know why that is.

The lights went down. The audience grew quiet. Mr. MacFadden gave Kate her cue, and she went out on the stage. When Mr. MacFadden opened the curtain and Sarah put on the stage lights, Kate was sitting onstage looking like an absolutely perfect Alice.

And she didn't say a word. She just looked out at the audience and her face got white as a sheet and she didn't say a single thing. Someone in the audience coughed. Kate looked backstage, right at me. I smiled at her. I gave her the thumbs-up sign. Nothing. "You can do it!" I mouthed.

Then she smiled back at me, and the color came into her face and she said, "Oh what is the use of a book, without pictures or conversations?"

After that, everything went perfectly. Well, almost perfectly. Charlie Goldstein's hat fell off while he was saying, "The Queen will chop off my head for being late," and everyone could see the big bandage on his forehead. But he just pointed right to it and said, "See! Last time she missed," and the audience laughed. Josh spilled water on my costume during the Tea Party scene, and Ellen's Tweedledum outfit split open in the middle of her poem about the Walrus and the Carpenter. But she didn't even giggle; she just kept right on going. I looked out into the audience whenever I could to see who was there, but it was so dark, I couldn't tell if my dad had made it or not.

Before I knew it, the play was over. I said my last line, "Off with her head!" and Kate said hers, "I guess it was all a dream," and then the lights went down, and the audience started clapping, and we all got up to take our bows.

It's the greatest feeling in the world when you hear a whole room full of people clapping and you know they're doing it for you. Everybody got a lot of applause, but Charlie Goldstein got a ton because people were so impressed that he went on with a broken arm. When it was time for Kate to take her bow, the audience started to clap even harder and yell, "Bravo!" And the nicest thing was that I didn't feel even a tiny little bit jealous of her. I just felt happy and proud. And I was particularly proud because Mr. MacFadden asked me to give her the flowers we had all chipped in for. I never saw her look as happy as she did standing there with her arms full of chrysanthemums (roses were way too expensive), bowing. I think I clapped harder than anybody. Afterward, the curtain fell and we all ran out into the audience, and there was a lot of hugging and kissing to do.

First we all hugged each other. I hugged Abby and Kate, and then Abby hugged Josh, and then Josh hugged me and Kate, which surprised us a lot, and then Ellen and Peggy stopped hugging each other and hugged me and Abby and Kate, and then Sarah and Pam came out and hugged everyone. I looked around for Charlie Goldstein to give him a hug, but I couldn't find him anywhere. Then all our parents came over to hug us and kiss us and tell us we were great. Even Alison gave me a big hug, which she doesn't do too much. The only thing that made me sad was that my father had missed the show.

"I'm sorry, honey," my mom said. "You know how much he wanted to come, but he got a call from the hospital this afternoon, and — "

Just then I looked up and saw my dad running into the auditorium. He must have rushed over right from the hospital.

"Did I miss it?" he called out. "I missed it, didn't I? Oh, Beth, I came as fast as I could."

"I guess you must have, dear," Mom said, looking down at his feet. He still had on those funny green slippers that doctors wear over their shoes in the hospital. He looked totally silly, but the thought of him rushing over so fast to see the play made me love him more than ever, and I gave him a giant hug and kiss.

"It's okay, Daddy," I said, laughing. "I understand."

Just then I saw Charlie Goldstein coming over with his parents. They weren't really very tall at all. In fact, he was already taller than his mother. But they both wore big round glasses just like his.

"I was wondering if you'd like to go to Aunt Emily's with me tomorrow," Charlie said. "My dad made a videotape of the whole play, and I thought we could show it to her."

"A videotape?" Dad said. "Now that's something I'd love to see." And he told the Goldsteins all about missing the performance, and everybody laughed again at his shoes. I was really glad that now he could at least see it on videotape.

The best thing that happened the whole night came later, though. After I had said good-bye to everyone, and we'd promised the Not For Blondes

Only club and their parents that we would all meet at Deli Delicious for a late sandwich, I went back to pick up my clothes and saw Mr. MacFadden picking up the dropped props off the floor and putting them into neat piles.

"Hi, Beth," he said. "Getting ready to go?"

"Yes, my parents are waiting in the car for me. I forgot my clothes," I said.

"You all did a great job tonight."

"Thank you."

"Thank *you*, Beth," he said. "You know, I wasn't sure if I could do *Alice in Wonderland* with your class. I mean, it's really a pretty hard show to do right. I knew I could find an Alice, but I didn't know if any of you could do the really tough parts, like the Queen of Hearts and the March Hare. But, then, I thought, 'Hey, Beth can do it.' I knew I could count on you, Beth. And you really did a wonderful job."

I was totally stunned. All along I had thought Mr. MacFadden had given me those parts because I wasn't good enough to play Alice. And now it turned out that he thought I was *too* good.

"Thank you," I said.

"I hope we can work together again," he said.

"Thank you," I said again. I sounded like a broken record.

"You're welcome, Beth," he said, laughing. "I know you were kind of mad at me for not giving you Alice, so I just wanted you to know why. Are we friends?"

"We're friends," I said.

"Good." He leaned over and kissed me on the cheek. "You're really a very talented actress, Beth."

"Thank you," I said one more time. I sounded like a dorfball. I didn't care, though. I didn't care about anything.

Later that night we were all at Deli Delicious, eating corned beef and listening to Vinnie complain about the new oven he'd gotten that keeps breaking down, when I looked out the window and saw Mr. MacFadden and Victoria, walking down the street arm in arm. They stopped at the corner and started kissing like there was absolutely no tomorrow, and I was just about to tell everyone when I stopped myself.

Because if you can't count on your friends to keep your secrets, then you can't count on them for anything.

About the Authors

Betsy Lifton and Karen Lifton have been sisters since birth. They have been writing as a team for many years, though the *Not* For Blondes Only books are their first novels. Betsy lives in Westchester County, New York, with her husband, son, and daughter. Karen lives in Buffalo, New York, with her husband and daughter. They are both brunette.

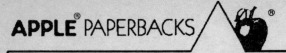

THE BABY-SITTERS CLUB®

Collect Them All!

by Ann M. Martin

The seven girls at Stoneybrook Middle School get into all kinds of adventures...with school, boys, and, of course, baby-sitting!

For a complete listing of all *The Baby-sitters Club* titles write to:
Customer Service at the address below.

Available wherever you buy books...or use this order form.

Scholastic Inc., P.O. Box 7502, 2931 E. McCarty Street, Jefferson City, MO 65102

Please send me the books I have checked above. I am enclosing $ _____
(please add $2.00 to cover shipping and handling). Send check or money order — no cash or C.O.D.s please.

Name _____

Address _____

City_____ State/Zip _____

Please allow four to six weeks for delivery. Offer good in U.S.A. only. Sorry, mail orders are not available to residents of Canada. Prices subject to change.   BSC192